AF653805

POPULAR

A Novel

POPULAR

A Novel

ALISSA GROSSO

JAICO PUBLISHING HOUSE

Ahmedabad Bangalore Bhopal Bhubaneswar Chennai
Delhi Hyderabad Kolkata Lucknow Mumbai

Published by Jaico Publishing House
A-2 Jash Chambers, 7-A Sir Phirozshah Mehta Road
Fort, Mumbai - 400 001
jaicopub@jaicobooks.com
www.jaicobooks.com

© Alissa Grosso

Published in arrangement with
Flux
an imprint of Llewellyn Publications
Woodbury, MN 55125 USA
www.fluxnow.com

POPULAR
ISBN 978-81-8495-422-7

First Jaico Impression: 2013

No part of this book may be reproduced or utilized in
any form or by any means, electronic or
mechanical including photocopying, recording or by any
information storage and retrieval system,
without permission in writing from the publishers.

Printed By
Anubha Printers
Plot No -19 Udyog Kendra Extn.-1,
Ecotech-III Greater Noida-201308

For my parents, who have always supported me.
The adventure continues ...

Part One

The CLIque

OLIVIA

Popularity has its privileges, but an ideal high school schedule isn't one of them. So, being the number two person to the number one girl in the school is not enough to save me from the sheer pointlessness of a mid-morning study hall in my senior year. In fact, being second in command does not entitle one to much of anything, like for instance knowing when your best friend is throwing her next party or who was lucky enough to make the guest list, as Chance Avanale proved when he burst through the door into study hall a good thirty or so seconds after the bell sounded, looking not contrite but more like someone who has just won the World Series. I guess that's kind of what it feels like.

Okay, so I've never once had to wonder whether or not

I would make Hamilton's guest list, or known the unmitigated thrill of seeing my name posted there for the very first time, but I do know that magic feeling of being chosen by the great Hamilton—although my magic moment came before anyone else's. Hamilton chose me all the way back in kindergarten.

The first day of school for a black girl at the blindingly white Fidelity Elementary was a terrifying experience. Also, I'd had the misfortune of attending a nursery school two towns away all because my aunt happened to be a teacher there. When, on that first day of class, the rest of the kids were picking up where they'd left off just a few months earlier, I was standing outside the circle looking in, a little girl with a scabbed knee and the wrong color skin who'd gone to the wrong school. There must have been others, I realize now, others who hadn't gone to that nursery school and who felt shy and nervous and left out, but I don't think I realized this then. As far as I could tell, I was the one and only outsider.

It's the sort of thing that can be traumatic at any age, let alone five. I remember crying, not in front of everyone because even at five I realized how fundamentally devastating that would have been, but later, as I was walking across the school's impossibly large front lawn toward my mother's waiting car. Not a bawling sort of cry, more a sappy movie cry. Tears of self-pity rolled down my cheeks and filled my eyes. Then, it happened.

The biggest, blondest, most beautiful girl in the class

was calling my name, knew my name. There, on the school's front lawn, she announced that we were going to be friends. Not asked, but told, and maybe if I'd been chosen later in life, I would have been indignant about the whole thing. Maybe, but probably not. Even at five, I sensed what this friendship would mean for me. Never once since have I stood outside a circle without it being my choice.

Is this really true? I mean, could it have happened exactly the way I think it did? I was five years old. How can I remember details like a skinned knee or tears on my cheeks? Then again, with such details, how can it not be true?

Anyway, what I know—looking at Chance striding toward his assigned seat with the world's broadest smile plastered across his face—is that I know the feeling. That elation. I've experienced it, and though it goes against every single cynical tendency I have, it's perhaps the greatest feeling ever.

The other thing I know is that I'm totally and completely smitten with Chance. This is not something I've just realized. In fact, I've spent the past year or so drooling over him, ever since I realized how he fills out his soccer jersey now instead of swimming in it. Ever since I realized that he suddenly looks a whole lot more like a young man than an oversized boy, I've had a monstrous crush on him. So I wonder, of course, if all my efforts to hide these feelings have been in vain, if Hamilton has somehow discovered my deepest, darkest desires and rewarded me by adding Chance to her first guest list of our senior year.

My heart is racing and my palms are sweating. Not because of Chance, but because I think Hamilton knows, and I don't want her to know. I don't want Hamilton involved. I want Chance. And I want him to be pure and untainted by Hamilton.

Some interminable time later, when the bell releases us from study hall hell, I'm walking down the hallway when behind me a voice calls, "Hey."

I feel lightheaded. I slowly turn around.

Chance smiles at me, slightly less broadly than when bolting into study hall announcing his good news to all who cared to hear, but it's still the smile of someone who is having a really, really good day.

"I just wanted to say thanks, you know," he says. "I mean about the guest list. I'm really looking forward to the party."

"Don't thank me," I say, then realize this sounds a bit snarky. "I mean, I'm glad you're on the guest list, and I'm looking forward to the party, too."

He nods, and God knows where the conversation might have gone from there, but I am suddenly yanked into the girls' bathroom by a disembodied hand.

Beneath the glow of dead-moth-encrusted fluorescent lights, I see that the hand belongs to none other than Shelly Trust. Unlike the beaming Chance, she's pouting like a spoiled little girl who didn't get a pony for her birthday. Moreover, the dirty green tiles of the bathroom floor and ceiling reflect off her pale skin and give her a look that borders on demonic. Dirty blond curls break free from their confinement in a glittering rhinestone barrette as she struggles to wedge a pilfered desk chair beneath the bathroom door handle, effectively giving us a private conference room.

"Next time, a polite 'excuse me' might work," I suggest.

"Can it, Olivia," she snarls. "Did you know about this?"

"Did I know about what? The existence of this bathroom?"

"Ha ha. You know goddamn well what I mean."

"Actually, I'm not sure that I do."

"You can't really be that oblivious. I'm talking about Hamilton posting a guest list."

"Oh, that," I say.

"Oh, that," she mimics in an unflattering voice. "Yes, that. Only the biggest news of the entire day, and I have to find it out from Melissa Drackett like some common idiot. I looked like a moron, Olivia."

"Somehow I don't think that had anything to do with Melissa or the guest list."

The door vibrates as if someone is trying to open it from the outside, but the chair holds. Someone shouts and then pounds on the door.

"Go away, bitch!" Shelly yells, then turns to me. "You knew about it, didn't you?" she demands. The pounding has stopped.

"I just found out about it in study hall."

"You're lying."

"Scout's honor," I say, and since I don't know the correct hand gesture, I cross my right hand across my chest with my middle finger extended. Shelly purses her lips and breathes loudly through her nose, now really looking like a demon.

"Did she or did she not consult you about this?" Shelly asks.

"I told you, I just learned about it a few minutes ago."

"That's insane. She's insane. Who the hell does she think she is, anyway? She's supposed to come to us about these things. We're supposed to talk things over. We're supposed to have some input into things."

"Says you," I say. "Hamilton never said that. I know for a fact."

Shelly's not like the rest of us. Not everyone realizes this, but I know it and Hamilton knows it, and it's possible Shelly knows it but she's such a complete airhead that I kind of doubt it. Shelly was not chosen. The rest of us were handpicked by Hamilton, but Shelly's the only one who chose Hamilton, who became a member of the clique on her own accord. I mean, in a sense Hamilton had to accept her, so it's not as if Shelly lacks Hamilton's blessing, but it's different with her, and maybe that's why I hate her.

I pull the chair out from beneath the door handle and start to open the door.

"Where are you going?" Shelly asks.

"To class."

"You really don't care, do you?"

"It wouldn't matter if I did."

As I'm walking out the door, I notice someone has written *EAT SHIT, HAMILTON* on the bathroom wall in black magic marker.

Shelly

Just because someone is the most popular girl in the school doesn't mean they will always be the most popular girl in the school. Hamilton thinks she's untouchable. She thinks that everyone will love her forever and ever. The problem is, she's sloppy and lazy and doesn't really know a goddamn thing about popularity. Just take one look at the losers she surrounds herself with. Anyway, popularity is something you've got to work at, and you've got to want it really, really bad. And I do.

This thing with the guest list may look trivial, but it's not just the fact that she didn't even bother to consult us that pisses me off. It's the fact that her guest list, frankly, sucks. There are people on that list who have no business being there, and really deserving people who should be invited to the party who aren't. If she had the courtesy to ask me ahead of time, to show me the list and ask my opinion of it, I could have pointed these flaws out to her, but no. Instead she just posts the thing for the world to see, and now her stupid list has become gospel.

"Well, I think it's kind of sweet that Tom is on it," says a voice I think belongs to Caitlin Rourke. I quickly slide into a stall so I can secretly listen to the rest of the conversation.

"Sweet maybe, but strange," says a second voice. Debbie Shune? "He's kind of a dork."

"I guess so, and it's weird that Rose didn't make the list, right?" says Caitlin.

"And Trevor. I'm telling you, it's like Hamilton was drunk or something when she made up that list."

Timing is everything, and so I pick that moment to step out of the stall. Debbie's mouth hangs open and she stands there looking at me like an idiot. Caitlin just smiles in that perky little way of hers.

"You might want to shut your mouth," I tell Debbie. "There's a lot of flies in here." Obediently, her mouth snaps closed.

"We were just joking around," Debbie says. "I wasn't being serious. I mean, it's kind of weird that Tom is on that list, but I can understand why Rose got left off."

"It's cool," I say. "Look, I agree. Trevor should be on there."

"He's really cute," Caitlin says.

I begin to examine myself in the bathroom mirror and pull some lip gloss from my purse; not that I need it, but

I need to show the girls that we're all friends and everything is fine. After a minute or so, they relax and begin to preen as well, and before long we're gossiping about who is cheating on whom and what was really going on in the back of the bus during last week's art-class field trip to the museum. This is the little stuff that Hamilton just doesn't get, and why I know her popularity isn't immortal.

The thing is, I've been a popular girl my whole life. In fact, up until the point I was so rudely uprooted from my home turf and replanted here in Fidelity, I was *the* popular girl. When a job transfer forced my family to move, I did not bury my head in the sand. I marched into Fidelity High with my chin up. It didn't take me long to figure out who called the shots, and I went right up to her. Even Hamilton, in her denseness, realized how special I was and brought me into her fold, into her clique of weirdos. Sometimes I'm grateful that things worked out so well, but other times I wonder if it would have been better if I'd never become one of the clique.

Knowing all that I know about Hamilton, I wonder if I couldn't have simply challenged her title as the most popular girl in the school and won, hands down. Instead I'm stuck in the role of glorified lackey while Hamilton still calls the shots.

I do have the inside advantage, and some empires are best toppled from the inside out.

Nordica

I name each shot in my head as I take it. This one is called Crushed Hopes. This one is called Freshman Discovers Popularity. They are the faces of my fellow students contorted with disgust, joy, shock, and envy. Later, I will develop each picture in my basement dark room, studying each face, trying to understand what it means to be that person at the moment in time when my shutter snapped closed, capturing them in a frozen instant of time.

I found the Nikon in my attic. It belonged to my grandfather a long time ago, and it's entirely manual. I took Intro to Photography last year and was the only student in the class who didn't have some fancy camera with bells and whistles galore. The other kids didn't get it when Mr. Hankins seemed to fawn over my camera, why he always held up my pictures as good examples and told me that I was gifted. For the other students, their camera was just another device in their gadget-filled life, just an appliance. They didn't have a special bond with their camera, as I did. They didn't understand how to look through the viewfinder and locate not just a pretty picture, but life itself with all its wrinkles.

There was a time when I would have felt self-conscious about wearing a camera around school all day. There was a time when I would have worried about what other people thought of me. Even after I became the youngest member of Hamilton's clique, I still spent an inordinate amount of time worrying about what people would think if I wore my hair differently, if I didn't dress in exactly the right clothes, if I said the wrong thing or did the wrong thing. Then, somewhere along the way, I realized that none of that stuff mattered. Or maybe I just found new things to worry about.

Anyway, somewhere along the way the rumor got started that I was on the yearbook committee. I don't know who started it, but I never went out of my way to dispel it. So nobody thinks it's the least bit odd that I go around school all day with a camera. They don't even care about me taking their picture, because after all, who wouldn't want to get their picture in the yearbook? Of course, none of these pictures will ever wind up in any yearbook. The only book they'll ever be in is my own private scrapbook, where page after page is filled with the faces of Fidelity High students captured in their most naked, most vulnerable moments.

When I get worried about the future, about what will happen to me when everyone else graduates, I pull out my scrapbook and flip through its pages. In part it's comforting to see those other faces, so many of them looking as troubled and scared as I feel. In part it's an effort to gain some understanding. Because as far as I can tell, next year it's going to fall to me to lead this flock of troubled souls, and I don't have a clue how to do this.

One face is conspicuously absent from my book, a face that will likely appear on every other page of the real yearbook. There are no pictures of Hamilton in my scrapbook, even though she is the most dominant figure in our high school and the most influential figure in my own life.

When I entered Fidelity High as a scared and pathetic freshman, I didn't have a clue who Hamilton was. My first day of school was a disaster. A mistake in the office had led to my schedule getting confused with that of a sophomore, and it took the better part of an hour to get things straightened out. I remember standing in the office near tears, pleading my case to the confused secretaries, when a pretty sophomore girl stepped into the office, immediately lighting up the room with her radiant blond hair and her bright blue eyes. Almost immediately she set things to rights.

"Wait a second," she said when the office computer finally spat out my correct schedule. "This won't work," she said.

"What's wrong?" I asked in a small, scared voice.

"They've put you in third lunch," she said. "And we always have second lunch."

Then, like that, she made the office ladies rearrange things so that I too could be in second lunch. And when we stepped out of the office, Hamilton was explaining where I would find their table in the cafeteria. I only thought I'd struck on a bit of good fortune to find someone willing to let me sit at their table during lunch. I didn't yet realize that it was much more than a lunch seating arrangement—that in those few minutes, Hamilton had decided I should join their clique. She'd adopted me and become my fairy godmother. In one moment I went from being a mousy little freshman with frizzy hair and braces to being one of the most popular girls in the school, who, inexplicably, had frizzy brown hair and wore braces.

That was the awesome power that is Hamilton. And so, perhaps, you understand why I'm so terrified about what will happen next year when she's gone.

Just look at the guest list pinned on a vacant bulletin board down in the desolate band wing of the school. Just a couple of sheets of paper, a list of names. Anyone could have printed up their own guest list and tacked it up there, but only Hamilton's list has the power to bring tears of joy and tears of devastation as popularity seekers alternately find or don't find their names on the sacred parchment.

A close-up of a cheek with mascara tear-streaks, as one unlucky soul learns that not today, not this week, and maybe not ever will she know what it is like to feel special, to feel envied. A shot of two friends hugging in relief as they find out they've both made the list. No awkward consoling for these two, no having to promise to not go to that stupid party anyway, then breaking that promise, because no matter how strong those friendship bonds are, you can't not go to Hamilton's party. And here's the boy who tries to look nonchalant, but the camera catches that gleam in his eye.

I know these people. I will pore over their faces for hours, later, in the privacy of my bedroom. I know them, but more importantly, they know me.

zelda

Three-plus years of taking the same path to the same table every single day, and my feet have probably worn a groove into the cafeteria's linoleum floor. I could find the table, our table, in my sleep, but as I walk that same path, there's a part of me that wants to break free from that pull.

The freaks sit over in the far corner. Goths, punks, and general malcontents. They've claimed a corner where they can be with their own kind and scoff at the rest of their classmates stuck in their little ruts. I want to sit in the far corner. I belong in the far corner. I'm a freak. That's my true identity, at least, but the freaks would never accept me. I'm tainted by the stain of popularity—I am one of the chosen ones. If I even tried to sit over there, if I even dared to talk to them, they would laugh in my face. They have every right to.

After all, just because Hamilton told me what to do

doesn't mean I had to listen. Hamilton knew all along that I would, though. That's why she picked me and not another freak—not, say, that girl over there with the purple hair, Carlotta I think her name is. Not her, because Carlotta would have told her what she could do with her stupid clique. Carlotta would have spat in her face and stomped on her foot and told her to leave her the fuck alone. But not Zelda Winston. Just because her wardrobe only contains shades of black and she cuts her hair in an unfashionable way, she's not *truly* weird. She just thinks she's a freak. She's a wannabe freak, and that's worse than not being a freak at all.

When I entered high school, I was determined to be an antisocial, anti-establishment little punk who nobody would mess with. I was the girl who got in trouble for building a shrine in her locker in eighth grade, complete with lit votive candles, to the lead singer of the latest goth band, for God's sake. So I was set to be hell-in-black-fishnet-stockings in high school, until popularity in the form of Hamilton Best came and shit on my parade. Since then, everything's been just peaches and cream and sunshiny daydreams.

The pisser is, I can't hate Hamilton. I was the one who took the bait. I was the one who had a sudden change of heart regarding my anti-establishment stance when I learned that the establishment wanted me. I went from revolutionary to dickhead politician at the drop of a hat, and I didn't look back.

Well, okay, sometimes I look longingly at the freaks

in their corner, but it's not for real. I know my place and so do my feet, and they carry me straight to it. I put down my tray and take my appointed seat.

"What's your opinion on all this, Zelda?" asks Shelly. She, Nordica, and Olivia have already begun their lunch and apparently some crucial discussion that only Shelly seems interested in.

"Opinion on what?" I ask.

"Zelda Winston, can you please join us in the land of reality. The guest list, damn it. What do you think about Hamilton just posting the thing without giving us so much as a courtesy heads-up?"

I'm not that out of it. I did overhear a conversation in the hallway about a new guest list being up, but it hadn't occurred to me that I should be hurt that Hamilton hadn't let us know ahead of time she was going to be posting a list.

"It's not really a big deal," I say.

"Told you," Olivia says.

"It seems like most people are really happy about it," Nordica says.

"What?" Shelly shrieks. "Who have you been talking to? The list is atrocious. Have you actually looked at it?"

"When's the party?" I ask.

"That doesn't matter. What matters is, there are a whole lot of people on that list that shouldn't be, and a whole bunch more who aren't, who should."

"Huh?" Olivia pretends to be confused. Maybe she

isn't pretending. Sometimes it sounds like Shelly is speaking a foreign language.

"The party's in October," Nordica volunteers. "It's a Halloween party."

"What?" Shelly says. "How do you know that?"

"'Cause that's what it says at the top of the list," Nordica says. "We should do some kind of themed group costume."

"Can we get back to the real issue here, and the fact that Hamilton doesn't think she needs to consult a single one of us when she does something this huge?" Shelly asks.

"What do I need to consult you about?" Hamilton suddenly appears behind Shelly.

"Your every bowel movement, if Shelly had her way," Olivia says.

"Olivia, this is a lunch table," Hamilton says.

"What about the Pink Ladies—you know, from *Grease*. We could get jackets made up." Nordica is still stuck on the whole group-costume idea.

"I don't wear pink," I say.

"Why are we getting jackets made up?" Hamilton asks.

"I was thinking we should go as some sort of themed thing for the Halloween party," Nordica explains.

"Maybe we should ask Hamilton's opinion," Shelly says. "What do you think, Hamilton? Do you want to do some sort matching costume or something that would tie in together, or should it be every woman for herself?"

"I've already got a costume picked out," Hamilton says. "The rest of you are on your own."

Hamilton

I've always thought that fall is the most depressing of seasons. The air reeks of death and decay and there's just this general air of finality, and this really is the final fall. Of high school, at any rate. Sure, I've graduated before. There was our fifth grade graduation when we moved on to middle school, and eighth grade graduation, with the whole stink-bomb fiasco, but high school is different because it really is the end. Oh sure, there's college and adulthood and all that, but it's just not the same. I think I knew all along that this was going to be a tough year, but I never realized just how soon it would get tough. I've already begun to tick off the milestones: last homecoming dance, last fall pep rally, last chocolate-bar fundraiser. It's only going to get worse as the year goes on.

As I walk down the path that leads from the teacher's

parking lot to the athletic fields, I try not to notice the fallen leaves that litter the ground, but the crisp autumn air and the accompanying reek of rot are not as easy to shut out.

"Hey, Hamilton!" I look up and see the boys' cross-country team heading toward me on a practice run, jogging by with the stealth of cats. I don't have time to step aside, and they move around me like a river around an island, all smiles and waves. It's stupid little stuff like this I'm going to miss.

Then I see him, the only person on that guest list who's an automatic given, and probably the only one on the list who doesn't give a damn. Alex is sitting on the bench at the bottom of the hill, and when I arrive, he stands up and takes my hand. I know some people don't see it, but as far as I can tell he's the most beautiful guy in the whole school. Tall and lean without being too skinny, and with a head of thick black hair that's always got that sexy messy look. He's as gorgeous as they come.

Then he smiles, and it's more than I can handle. He's the perfect guy—charming, attentive, and understanding. He knows me better than anyone. I can't imagine life without Alex. I find it hard to believe that I ever lived without him. I don't know what will happen to us when we graduate. I mean, it's not as if we'll break up the second we're done with school, but high school relationships don't usually survive the going-away-to-college thing. That's what scares me more than anything about leaving. School, friends, the whole thing is nothing compared to Alex, and

I would give it all up in a heartbeat if I knew it meant never having to lose him. But it doesn't work that way.

We walk hand in hand down the path, two lovers out for an autumn stroll. To an observer we look peaceful, idyllic even, but what an observer doesn't know is that one half of the pair is a nervous wreck inside, scared to even breathe lest she somehow upset the whole delicate balance of the universe.

"Hamilton?"

"Yeah," I say.

"I was just wondering how you're doing. You seem quiet," Alex says.

See what I mean about him being a perfect guy?

"They all hate me," I say.

"By all, you mean everyone on the planet?"

"Practically. I think at least the whole school."

"Well, I don't hate you," he says.

"Okay, half the school, but the whole clique."

"And you don't think maybe you're exaggerating?"

"They're pissed about the guest list, because I didn't consult them on it. Because they don't agree with it."

"And they hate you because of this?"

"Well, maybe not all of them, but Shelly definitely. Shelly hates me."

"Shelly Trust?" Alex scoffs. "You're upset because of what Shelly Trust thinks?" Alex hates Shelly, and the feeling's pretty much mutual. He's apparently not the right guy for me to date, in Shelly's mind; he tarnishes my image or something like that. Anyway, I see Alex's point about me getting upset over this. It's stupid.

"It's not just that," I say. "It's been hitting me, you know. High school coming to an end."

"Not that again. You can't be depressed about that, for God's sake. It's our senior year. The best year of them all. The whole year is like one big party, and nobody knows how to throw a party like Hamilton."

"Speaking of which, for my Halloween party would you be willing to be Peter Pan to my Tinker Bell?"

"Only if we get to stay forever in Never Never Land."

I wish there were such a place. I wish it was here, now. I want to live in this moment forever, here with Alex walking along a path in the shadow of the school. I want to stay here always, in this, our last year of high school, the best year of our lives. I don't want to grow up. I don't want any of this to change.

OLIVIA

I'm not in my Halloween costume, though I do look frighteningly like my Aunt Dee in this flowered head scarf and ridiculously chunky pair of sunglasses. Is all this necessary? Probably not, but when Alex asked me to meet him at the library, he said he wanted to keep things hush-hush, whatever the hell that means. He never bothered to tell me why he wanted to meet me there, and I can only assume it has something to do with the big shindig tonight, but what Alex Journer could possibly have to say to me regarding Hamilton's party I can't imagine. And of a hush-hush nature, no less.

I see his lanky body stride purposefully across the library floor. It's hard to believe that this is the boy dating the most popular girl in our high school. He looks like someone who should be nothing but your common-variety loser. Not that I believe in stereotypes, I don't, but with all the guys Hamilton has to choose from, it's weird that she chose Alex. Okay, most days I have a hard time understanding how any girl in the school could choose anyone other than Chance.

"Olivia?" Alex says in a breathless sort of voice, as if he has just run all the way here.

"Right, my disguise is just so good, you couldn't tell," I say.

He makes a strange little gasping noise that I realize is a sort of single-syllable chuckle. I imagine Alex a few decades down the road, some creepy old guy who spends his days in the library checking out all the high school girls that walk in, gasping out his little creepy laughs. If anyone is daring enough to engage him in conversation, he'll bore them with stories of his glory days, about dating the most popular girl in the school, how he lost her when she found someone better or went away to school or maybe just decided that her boyfriend would likely turn out to be a creepy old man some day.

Alex pulls out the chair across from me at the table and sits down. He can't seem to get comfortable as he folds and unfolds his hands, lays them flat on the table, folds them again, all the while crossing and uncrossing his legs and engaging in a floor-vibrating amount of foot tapping.

I want him to ask if I find any of this annoying so that I can respond with a resounding yes, but instead Alex says, "I'm worried about Hamilton."

I wonder if my daydream was some sort of prescient

warning of the future, and if Alex somehow realizes that his relationship with the Great One is just a fluke. Has he sought me out as a confidante in the hopes that I'll be able to have some sort of heart-to-heart conversation with Hamilton, some television-movie-like moment where we spill our hearts and souls out to one another? Perhaps, as well as he knows Hamilton, he doesn't realize that I don't have a relationship like that with Hamilton. Hamilton just isn't that sort of person, and maybe I'm not either.

"She thinks you guys hate her," he says. "The clique."

"I don't hate her," I say. But it takes me too long to say it, like I had to think about it, which I did, but I'm hoping Alex doesn't hear it that way.

"She's worried about graduation," Alex says.

"She's afraid she's going to trip on her gown and stumble down the aisle?"

"She doesn't want high school to end."

"She always has been a bit of a closet masochist."

Alex just gives me a look with those dark, brooding eyes of his. I notice that his eyebrows are too big, verging on bushy. He needs to watch them or he'll end up a creepy old guy with creepy extra-bushy eyebrows. He's trying to be all serious, and apparently doesn't appreciate the fact that I don't see things quite the way he does. The problem with people like Alex is they're always looking for everything to be some sort of portentous, dramatic event, when in reality, in terms of the big picture, most things don't matter all that much.

He's worried about Hamilton? She's the last person on

earth that needs worrying about. She's got it all together. She's the most in-control person I've ever known. Oh boo hoo, Hamilton's sad about high school coming to an end. From my experience, Hamilton being sad about high school coming to an end only means that Hamilton will somehow figure out a way to remedy the situation. Somehow or other, she'll ensure that high school doesn't come to an end, or that the lifestyle that she's so fond of just goes on and on forever. I don't expect Alex to understand all this. He's only known her a couple of years, but if the two of them stay together long enough, he'll see how senseless it is to worry about Hamilton because no matter what she wants, she's going to find a way to get it.

It's the rest of us who really need the pitying, because more than anything, the end of high school means the end of the clique, and for its members that means the end of Hamilton's seemingly divine powers over our lives. Like it or not, we've been spoiled for a long time, some of us longer than others. When this is all over, we'll be left on our own, tackling the world without any special powers to help us along the way. Now *that's* something to be worried about.

As much as I've always dreamed of someday being something other than Hamilton's lackey, I've never actually managed to conceive of a life for myself beyond her reach. What happens after high school? I don't know. I can't really imagine what will happen, what it will be like. College? If I went to a different college than Hamilton, and it's more than likely that I would, how would I survive? Not since nursery school have I experienced a school environment that was lacking in Hamilton. Not since nursery school have I ever been anything other than Hamilton Best's best friend.

"She may not talk about it much," Alex says, "but it's eating away at her."

"You don't think maybe this is a bit of transference," I say. "You don't think maybe it's *you* who's scared about high school ending, and you losing the greatest thing that ever happened to you?"

"What's that supposed to mean?" I think at first he's pissed at me for pointing out that Hamilton is the greatest thing that's ever happened in his loser life, but even he seems quite willing to admit this is true. "You think that just because we're not in school together, we're going to break up?"

"Maybe not right away, but Hamilton's a proactive person. When it's time for her to move on, she's going to. Completely. She'll leave us all in the dust. You know that, don't you?"

"Not you," he says to the table top. He looks so sad, like a sulking little boy. Maybe I shouldn't have said anything, even if it was true.

"I've got to get going," I tell him. "I still haven't put together my costume for tonight."

"My mom dyed my jeans green," he says. I wonder what he's going as. The Jolly Green Giant?

"Hey, Alex," I say in a forced-casual kind of way as I gather up my stuff. "Do you know Chance Avanale at all?"

The question forces him out of his sulk, or at least makes him look up at me.

"He plays soccer," he says.

"Yeah, I know. I was just wondering if you knew him at all."

I know it's a stretch. Alex is a loner by nature, and if he's hanging out with others of his gender, it's not the Chances of the world.

"Why?" he asks, and he looks angry, maybe even hurt. I'm sure I've hit upon some sore point. No doubt Chance kicked sand in his face in first grade or gave him a wedgie or some other stupid boy thing.

"Well, you know he made the guest list, and I was just wondering what kind of guy he was. He seems really nice, you know."

"He's not that nice," Alex says. "He's not that nice at all." Okay, definitely some long-held resentment there; perhaps there was a whole series of wedgies.

"Right. Well, okay then. I'll see you later."

I start to walk away, but Alex says, "Hey, what's your costume going to be?"

"I was thinking of going as a disaffected teenage girl or maybe a zombie."

Shelly

The Trust family has always been a respectable, upper-middle-class family, and back when we lived in a town with a country club we were, of course, among its most prominent members. But in a town like Fidelity, which is admittedly quite a bit beneath us, we have not had the luxury of belonging to any social clubs and have had to make do with the recreations of the locals, such as they are. I tell you all this so that you can understand where I'm coming from. Let's just say Hamilton's parties are simple affairs that, with the right attitude, can be fun, but they're hardly the sort of social events one will look back on with any degree of fondness.

When I first befriended Hamilton and entered her motley circle of friends, I urged her to allow me to handle the party preparations. I have experience in this area and know I could host an affair that would be light years above anything the youth of this town have ever seen. But Hamilton is set in her ways and insists that she knows how to throw a party. So, our role as Hamilton's faithful hangers-on is to come over to her house a few hours ahead of time to help move furniture and decorate.

We've all come in costume, well, those of us who have any sense of fun, that is. I'm glittered up from head to toe as Glinda the Good Witch, and I look, if I do say so myself, absolutely stunning. Nordica, the poor thing, did her best with a long blond wig braided with gold ribbon and a medieval-type gown too low-cut for her uncurvaceous body. She's either Rapunzel or Guinevere, I'm not sure which, and I sincerely doubt that she knows either. Zelda has gone as a witch, how original, and if truth be told, she doesn't look much different than she does every other day of the week, with the exception of the pointed hat and the pasted-on nose wart. Olivia is wearing no costume but tells us that she's a zombie. As for her highness herself, she's been locked in the bathroom getting ready since we got here.

"What's this?" I ask, pulling two packages from the party-supply store bag. It was a huge mistake to leave Zelda in charge of buying the decorations.

"It's streamers," Zelda explains. "To hang from the ceiling and stuff."

"I can see that, but where's the orange? Everyone knows that Halloween colors are black and orange." The packages contain one roll of black crepe paper and one roll of purple.

"But aren't black and orange the colors for St. Paul's?" Nordica asks.

"This is not about school spirit," I explain. "This is about Halloween."

"Purple seems as much like a Halloween color as orange, if you ask me," Olivia says.

"Well, nobody asked you," I say, "and frankly, I don't see why we should take Halloween advice from someone who can't even bother to wear a costume."

"I'm a zombie," Olivia explains.

"If you say that one more time, I'm dumping the punch over your head, I swear to God," I say. People just don't appreciate what I put up with from these morons.

"At least I didn't come dressed as the good witch of the north," Olivia says. "You look like a sequin shop exploded."

"I suppose in all fairness," I counter, "you do have the scariest looking costume in the room."

"Um, maybe somebody could help me hang the streamers," Zelda says.

Of course, the whole thing is a disaster. The decorations look like crap. There's nowhere near enough food, and all of it looks barely edible. At least I stopped at the bakery to buy a bunch of Halloween cookies; everything else has the look of a church potluck supper. Then, of course, there's the fact that we have the whole place decorated and ready, with guests set to arrive any moment, and Hamilton hasn't even bothered to come out of the bathroom.

"I think maybe someone should go check on her," Nordica says. "She could be sick."

"I'll cast a get-well spell," Zelda says, and begins dancing around the room and chanting something that I can only assume is an actual Wiccan spell. Nobody else seems alarmed that she knows some weird chant, as if there's nothing at all bizarre about her behavior.

"Stop it!" I yell, and at that very moment Hamilton walks in.

She looks great, and it's not hard to see why it took her so long to get ready. Her short little dress fits her perfectly, and her large, perfect wings look like something from a Broadway show. She must have gotten them from a costume shop. She's covered her arms and legs in an iridescent body glitter, and her hair, swept up and curled, also shimmers beneath the living room light. Her makeup is perfect, and I can't help but notice the way her angel costume and my Glinda costume seem to go so perfectly together. This is what they mean when they say that great minds think alike. Hamilton and I are birds of a feather.

"Olivia," Hamilton says, "costumes are not optional."

"I'm a zombie," Olivia says.

I'm looking over at the punch bowl, but just then the doorbell rings, and so both Hamilton and I are unable to deliver Olivia a satisfactory rebuke.

Nordica

Standing on the fourth stair up, I'm close enough to hear everything going on but just removed enough to look down at it all as an uninvolved observer. I'd wanted to bring my camera, but I couldn't figure out how to tie it into my costume. It's just, Hamilton always throws the best parties. Next year, when I'm on my own, I'll have to play hostess. I know my parties will never be as good as Hamilton's, but if they could be just half as good, I would be happy.

There is music playing—a collection of songs, some Halloween-themed, some not, that Hamilton handpicked just for the party. Some of the kids are dancing in the living room, which has been emptied of most of its furniture. Alex is in the center of the dancing kids, laughing and having a good time. He's dressed, I think, as Robin Hood, and he looks good out there, especially when he smiles. He's cute, not traditional Hollywood-handsome, but cute in a boy-next-door kind of way. I mean, it's not like I have a crush on him or anything—well, maybe just a small one. It's just, I understand why Hamilton is so crazy about him. If I had a boyfriend who was just half as fun and good-looking as Alex, I would be happy.

If I had a boyfriend, I would be happy.

"Quit hiding. Come join the party." It's Olivia in her costume-less costume. She and a sophomore boy named Frank something-or-other were the only two people to dare show up without at least making an attempt at a costume.

"I was just watching things," I say, realizing I'm still looking at Alex in the center of the makeshift dance floor. Olivia follows my gaze and I can't help blushing, but I don't think she notices.

"Who's the gorilla?" she asks, pointing at a costumed figure doing an improvised disco dance.

"I'm not sure," I say. "I haven't seen him without a mask."

She heads downstairs, and I watch as she walks out onto the dance floor, past the dancing and smiling Alex, toward the gorilla, but the gorilla has turned around and is leaving the room. I decide that maybe now would be a good time to go downstairs. To join the party, as Olivia says.

zelda

For those of us on the fringe, Halloween is far and away the best holiday. It's the one day of the year when we look like normal people, for one. Costumes liberate people, and Hamilton's annual Halloween party is always the best of her parties. People are so much more fun when they're uninhibited. People will do things when they're wearing a mask that they won't do any other time.

Hamilton's finished basement has become the game room for tonight's festivities. Sasha Baker, who came dressed as a Playboy bunny, is at the center of a slightly modified game of Pin the Tail on the Donkey, her ass serving as the target, with guy after guy lining up to try and stick her powder puff of a tail onto its intended target. It's all very funny, and there's such a minimal amount of alcohol and recreational drugs involved that it really gives you hope for this new generation. I'm sitting on the couch enjoying the whole scene when the gorilla appears, and then for some reason I feel uneasy.

I can't remember having any sort of childhood trauma involving gorillas, but perhaps there was some bad day at the zoo that I've blotted from my conscious memory. That would be the only thing that could explain why I feel so uneasy with the costumed creature. I don't know who it is—a boy, I assume, because gorilla costumes are not the sort of thing that girls normally wear. But since the gorilla hasn't said anything or bothered to take off his mask, I don't know who it is.

Not that removing his mask would necessarily clear things up. It's true, I live in my own world and don't stay up on who's who at Fidelity High. If I really need to find out who someone is, I just need to consult Shelly and she'll tell me their name, address, favorite color, and what they ate for breakfast. So, as annoying as she can be, she's good to have around once in a while.

I know it's just one of my classmates in a gorilla costume, and all I have to do is go over to him, find out who it is, and realize that all this stupid feeling-uncomfortable business, even maybe feeling a little scared, is all ridiculous. So, I get up and am about to go over to the gorilla when someone grabs my shoulder. As the gorilla walks away, the hand on my shoulder digs in its talons. I turn around to find Shelly Trust and her manicured fingernails locked onto the shoulder of my black gown.

"I need to talk to you," she hisses.

"Give me five minutes," I say, watching the two hairy legs ascending the basement staircase.

"No. Now. It's urgent."

"Okay, fine, talk." I realize I'm just going to have to catch up with the gorilla later. "And let go of my shoulder."

"Not here, some place private. The bathroom."

The basement bathroom is a closet-sized room that only barely accommodates one person comfortably. It's ridiculously cramped with two of us in there.

"I have my doubts about how important this all is," I say.

"Oh, well, did you know there's someone here who isn't supposed to be here?" Shelly asks.

"It's me. I'll leave. I'm having difficulty breathing in here anyway."

"Don't get cute. I've done a head count, and there's one too many people at this party."

"You've been counting people? Jesus, Shelly, it's a party. You're supposed to be having fun."

"Something felt off to me. So, I decided to investigate."

I think about the gorilla. Was he looking at her too, I wonder?

"Okay, so who's the extra person?"

"It's tough to say. I'm not sure who everyone is with the costumes, but clearly someone is at this party who wasn't on the guest list."

"Maybe someone brought a date," I say, "a sophomore or someone who wasn't aware of the strict guest list rules."

Personally, I hate the guest list rules. I don't know

why Hamilton needs to be so restrictive. Okay, I realize that this is her mom's house, and she doesn't want things to get out of hand and get too destructive, but still, not including people seems so unfair. It's too much like some sort of snobbish club, although thankfully it's Hamilton drafting the list, and she knows how to pinpoint just the right mix of people. Were Shelly at the helm, I can only imagine the shallow, insipid group of popularity goons she would assemble. If Shelly were writing the list, I probably wouldn't be here.

"Maybe you should start checking IDs," I say, joking.

"I was thinking about that, but I noticed that a lot of the girls came without their purses, which means they probably don't even have their ID with them."

"Does it really matter that much? I mean, so what if there's an extra person here. He or she isn't causing any sort of problem, right? The party's going just fine. So who cares."

"Somebody's here who shouldn't be. It's not fair—why should they get to have a good time? They weren't invited."

"Okay, fine." I can't breathe.

I step out of the bathroom, and Tyler Pittman, who apparently has just been crowned the winner of Pin the Tail on the Bunny, waggles his eyebrows at me.

"Hey," he says. "I'm the winner and get to go first in Five Minutes in the Closet, what do you say?"

"I've got to go see a gorilla about a horse," I say, and head upstairs.

Hamilton

Inside the house, the party's still in full swing, and everyone's having a great time. I stand on the patio listening to the sound of happiness that emanates from the house and know that I'm responsible for it. It feels good. I want every party I throw this year to be perfect, and so far I'm off to a good start. Still, I can't help thinking that it's one less party to look forward to. Before I know it, I'll be planning the big end-of-the-school-year party.

"There you are." I turn to see Alex stepping out onto the patio. "Well, you've outdone yourself once again."

"It is a good party, isn't it?"

"Fantastic," he says. "Which begs the question, why aren't you in there enjoying it?"

"I just needed some fresh air." I look up at the sky, which is clear, the stars all bright gemstones overhead.

"It's a nice night," he says. "In fact, it's a perfect night for dancing beneath the stars."

He holds out his hand, and I take it, so warm, so welcoming. I love him, but it's hard when you love someone so much you're scared of losing him. We slow dance beneath the stars, on the patio, at first to a tune that Alex hums, and then to a tune that drifts out to us in snatches from inside.

When the dance is through, we sit cuddled together on the cold cement of the patio. With Alex's arms around me, I don't feel so cold, even though I have nothing on but a skimpy little dress.

"Now, Tink," he says, "you're still not all hung up on the end of high school and everyone hating you, are you?"

"I still wish this really was Never Never Land."

"Well, who doesn't." He kisses me sweetly behind my ear and it sends a shiver through my whole body, but I'm still not cold.

"Shelly told me there's an extra person here. She's apparently been counting people," I say.

"She's counting people? What's wrong with her?"

"She said something felt wrong. So, she counted and came up with one too many people."

"Didn't Shelly fail math last year?" Alex asks.

"Yeah, but this isn't algebra we're talking about, this is basic kindergarten counting."

"I wouldn't trust Shelly to count her own fingers."

I laugh, even if it is mean.

"We don't check people off at the door, but maybe we should."

"Uh, Hamilton, this is a party. Even if there was some extra person here, which I sincerely doubt, I would just take it as a compliment. Obviously they know the best place in town to be on a Saturday night. I don't know why you care so much about what Shelly thinks. She's the devil."

"Glinda the Good Witch, actually. Tom Leahy is the devil. With all the costumes, anyone could be here. Like, who is that in the gorilla outfit anyway?" Alex lets go of me then, and the full coldness of the night hits me in the form of a light breeze that penetrates right down to my bones. I hug my knees to my chest but can't help shivering.

"That's Chance," he says. "He's on the list."

"Yeah, you're right, he is," I say. I'm a little bit shocked—Alex is usually oblivious to who is and is not on the list. "I think I'm going to go inside. It's freezing out here."

"Yeah," he agrees. But he doesn't follow me in right away.

OLIVIA

The gorilla led me on a merry chase, and I might have spent the rest of the night chasing him around. Certainly I wouldn't have noticed Chance in the kitchen if I hadn't walked right into him. In his fake leopard-skin outfit with half his chest bare, it was amazing that I hadn't noticed him.

"Chance," I say, startled, completely embarrassed that I made myself look like an idiot by walking into him.

"Me Tarzan," he corrects me.

"Of course you are," I say. "How silly of me not to have noticed. Was that by chance one of your ape friends passing through here a few seconds ago?"

"Everyone keeps asking that, but I'm not sure who the big monkey is. Hey, by the way, this is one awesome party."

"Yeah, it's not bad," I agree, mentally adding that for me,

anyway, it has improved a hundredfold in the past few seconds.

"Um, I know it's not exactly football or anything, but the soccer team's been doing pretty good this year," Chance says. "In fact, we made the district playoffs. So, if you're not doing anything next weekend, you should come down and cheer us on. Oh, and bring lots of friends, because we're playing St. Paul's and we're going to need all the support we can get."

"Yeah, that sounds like fun."

"Well, really it's mostly just sitting there watching a bunch of guys run up and down a soccer field, but who knows, we might actually win."

I can't think of a better way to spend my time than to watch Chance run up and down a soccer field. His eyes are a blue-green color, and I am getting warm and kind of dizzy staring into them. I want to say something, anything to keep the conversation going, but I can't think of anything intelligent to say. I can't think, period. It's like, just standing next to Chance, he sends out these vibes that scramble all my thoughts.

"So, um," I begin, not so intelligently.

"Hey, Chance! Quit flirting and get your butt out on the dance floor!"

We both look over. Donna Lukowski is standing in the hallway with a hand on her hip expectantly. Panic seizes me. Are they an item? I didn't think so, but high school romances are the sort of thing that come and go so quickly, it's hard for the apathetic to keep track. Donna marches up to him, grabs his arm, and drags him away with her, while he turns back to me, shrugging and looking a bit apologetic, but not, in my opinion, apologetic enough.

Donna Lukowski? If they really are a couple, then he's a complete ignoramus. She's nothing but an obnoxious little tart. If that's the sort of girl he's interested in, then I'm shit out of luck. But he did invite me to his soccer game. That has to count for something, doesn't it? Only he told me to bring lots of friends, which doesn't exactly make for an intimate and romantic moment. Yes, and he did indicate what he was looking for was a cheering section. So, of course, if you needed a cheering section, wouldn't you ask the girl who was best friends with the most popular girl in the school to bring all the friends she could? Of course, if you actually took the time to get to know that girl, you might realize that she wasn't someone that made friends with everyone, that she didn't act like the Shelly Trusts of the world, who use their popularity to draw people to them like moths to a porch light. In fact, if you took the time to get to know this girl, instead of shaking your thang out there on the dance floor with Donna Lukowski of all people, you might realize that she had exactly four friends, and one of them was Shelly Trust, a girl she could barely stand.

"Olivia, there you are, I've been looking all over for you," Shelly says, grabbing hold of my arm as if she were using it to pull herself up a cliff face.

"Let go of my arm."

"Don't be so touchy," Shelly says, letting go.

"You were the one who was touching me."

"Whatever. Have you seen our favorite angel lately?"

"Who the fuck is our favorite angel?"

"Hamilton, of course." Shelly exhales loudly through her nose to show her exasperation, but it sounds more like the noise of a frustrated farm animal.

"Since when has she become a heavenly messenger?"

"Her Halloween costume, you twit."

I love it when Shelly calls me a twit when she's the one who's the idiot. Thankfully for me, that happens a lot.

"She's dressed as Tinker Bell. Alex is Peter Pan," I inform her.

"Fine. Whatever. Just answer the goddamn question."

"I haven't seen her in a while."

"I can't find her," Shelly says. "You don't have a copy of the guest list, do you?"

"Oh yeah, right here in my back pocket."

"Thank God." Shelly holds out her hand expectantly as I roll my eyes. "Give it over."

"I wasn't serious. I don't have a copy of the guest list. I have never had a copy of any guest list, and come to think of it, I've never had a reason to have a copy of any guest list, ever."

"You know, it's clear from the way you're dressed that you didn't even want to be here anyway. So why don't you do us all a favor and go home?"

What I said before, about only having four friends and one of them being Shelly? Let me now amend that statement. What I meant to say is that I only have three friends.

"Should I click my heels three times, Glinda?" I ask.

"No, you should fuck off."

Have you ever known someone who you're pretty sure was only put on this planet to make your life a living hell? That's Shelly. Even if she could learn to keep her big mouth shut and act like a normal human being, she would still look like Shelly and that would be enough to make me sick to my stomach. I don't know why Hamilton doesn't just excommunicate her. About the only thing she's good for is staying up on the latest gossip, and since I don't care about that, it's not much of an asset in my opinion.

Correction. I almost never care about the latest gossip.

"Hey, do you know if there's something going on between Donna and Chance?" I ask her.

"Do you always have to be such a wise-ass?"

"I'm serious."

"Please, Donna's been head over heals for Chance since kindergarten," Shelly says.

"You didn't live here in kindergarten."

"And you did. That's why it's beyond sad that you're asking me about this. So, what happened? Were they getting frisky on the sofa? I want all the details."

"They were dancing," I say.

"And?"

"And Donna was so wasted, she pissed her pants right on the dance floor and Chance had to take her to the bathroom to help her clean herself up."

"No way!"

"Saw it with my own two eyes."

"Oh my God!"

Suddenly, Shelly has very pressing business in another room. I'm confident that everyone in the school will have heard the story about Donna's accident by first period Monday morning. If I'm lucky, she won't make the next guest list.

Shelly

There's nothing more depressing than being at a party after it's over. It's unavoidable as a hostess, and so I suppose that's what makes party-goer the more enviable position. An hour after the last guest departed, we were still picking up spent paper plates and napkins that had been left, hidden all over the house like Easter eggs. Honestly, people are such pigs. At least now an end was in sight. Zelda was at the sink scrubbing what needed scrubbing, and Olivia had already wheeled the vacuum cleaner out of the closet.

"Well, I thought the party turned out really great," Nordica says. "Everyone had a great time, I think."

"They come to a party expecting to have fun," I explain. "So, barring any really tragic circumstances, they are going to have fun. People having fun is not the mark of a really good party."

"Then what is?" Nordica asks.

"Yes, Shelly, do tell, what is the mark of a really good party, if it's not people having fun?"

Hamilton had crept into the room, silent as a cat, and once again caught me in a compromising statement.

"People almost always have fun at parties," I say. "What separates a really good party from an only okay one is that it's the sort of party people will still remember and still talk about years from now."

"Have you been reading Emily Post again?" Hamilton asks. "Shelly, we're in high school. Not every party has to rival the bashes thrown at Gatsby's mansion."

"Is he that sophomore whose dad made all that money on the Internet company?" Nordica asks.

"You're thinking of Brian Desai," I say. "Who by the way, Hamilton, is someone you might want to consider for the next guest list. He would certainly make a lot more sense than some of the people at this party."

"Gatsby is a character from a novel," Hamilton says, "who made a lot of money like Brian Desai's dad, then found out that money wasn't enough to buy him love and happiness."

I'm guessing the remark is a dig at me, but I don't bite. She really underestimates me if she thinks she can get under my skin that easily. Hamilton is, shall we say, sensitive about the whole money thing. She isn't trailer trash or anything, but this house is what a realtor might describe as "cute." We're not talking about someone who's used to living the good life. I've got a lot more money than she does, than any member of the clique does, and I think sometimes that's a sore point. Though I have magnanimously offered to host parties, to use the connections I have through my parents, to more or less share the wealth, I am always firmly rebuffed. It would be ridiculous for someone to resent me because of my wealth, but I know sometimes Hamilton, and Olivia too, I think, really have a hard time accepting our unequal economic positions.

I hate hearing stupid, over-repeated phrases like "money doesn't buy happiness." Well, of course you can't just walk into a store and pick up a five-pound bag of happiness, but if you think in a metaphorical kind of way, money can and does buy happiness. Money is what pays for the roof over our head and the clothes on our back. Money is how we buy all of our food. So, if we didn't have money, we would be homeless, naked, and hungry. But with it, we're doing great. It's not easy to be happy when you don't know where the next meal is coming from. Take a look around you. The happy people in this world are not the ones with financial problems, just hanging on until their next paycheck. Money doesn't buy happiness, my ass.

"This is good enough for tonight," Hamilton says. "I'll make a final pass-through tomorrow."

"I don't mind staying," Nordica says, playing up the lackey role just a bit too much for my taste.

"Not now, Nordica," Hamilton says. "Your presence is requested in the kitchen, and you too, Shell."

I have visions of us helping to dry and put away dishes, assembly-line fashion, but instead I'm greeted by a darkened kitchen lit only by the flickering orange flames of a few votive candles set out on the table.

"Zelda, is this your idea?" I ask. "Are we calling spirits?"

"Speaking of spirits," says Olivia, raising a hand to her brow and squinting at me, "I think I see the decrepit form and hear the discordant voice of the ghost of Halloween past—either that or it's just Shelly."

"Ha ha," I say, unimpressed. "Seriously, what the hell is this?"

"Don't look at me," Zelda says. "I was just washing the dishes."

"I lit the candles," Hamilton says, and joins us as we all stand around the table waiting for her cue. "Before long, we'll all be moving on and heading our own separate ways, but we'll all have this, the best time of our lives. We'll carry the memory of these days with us in our hearts wherever we go."

"When exactly did I fall into a treacle factory?" Olivia asks.

"Olivia, I'm not above setting your stupid unfestive shirt on fire with one of these candles," Hamilton says.

"Fine, go on. I'll carry the memory of your threat in my heart."

"Bitch," I say.

"I just wanted to take a moment to recognize how significant this year will be for us," Hamilton says, continuing as if Olivia hadn't gone and spoiled the moment. "There are a finite number of memories left to be made this year, and we need to remember to cherish each and every one."

"That's so beautiful," I say, but really I think the whole thing is just too weird. It doesn't make any sense. Why go through all this crap? She can't really believe it, can she? There has to be some sort of explanation.

Then I understand. This whole goddamn charade is on my account. I don't know how she knows, but she knows. Maybe she saw me talking to Debbie and Caitlin earlier at the party. Maybe some rumor reached her through one of a hundred possible channels. Somehow she knows that I am prepared to strike out on my own, to make my own way in the world of high school popularity. In other words, to directly challenge her claim to the throne. It is bold, brazen, a touch duplicitous and completely and totally deserved. It is overdue, really. I have been nothing but good and loyal to Hamilton for three years, but rather than be rewarded, I am treated like crap, overlooked. Certainly she doesn't view me as an equal, and that is unacceptable. I am just planning on claiming the respect that is rightfully mine.

I didn't count on Hamilton finding out so soon, but I should have realized that she has ways of finding out just about anything, at least as it relates to the students of Fidelity High School. I don't care that she knows. She would have known sooner or later, anyway. I just had hoped it would be at least a little bit later, when my position was firmly established, but no matter.

I am certainly not going to be moved by this ridiculous

speech about cherishing memories. What utter and complete bullshit. If she thinks this is the sort of thing that's going to make me see things in a whole new light, she's severely underestimated me. But then, she always has, hasn't she?

"Everyone, please take a candle," Hamilton says. There are five votives on the table and we each lift one, holding the lit candles carefully to avoid spilling hot wax on ourselves. "Together, our five candles are going to light the center candle, symbolizing our unity. Okay, ready?" I'm wondering if she will do an on-your-marks-get-set-go kind of thing, but no such luck. "Okay, now." The five of us stretch our candles, which are now dripping wax onto the table, toward the tall taper candle in the center, where our flames meet and briefly join to light it.

We draw the candles back and stand there holding them beneath our faces, looking a bit like kids telling ghost stories around a campfire. Except for Nordica, whose candle has gone out. Well, I always did think she was a little dim. I think this is a great line and really want to say it out loud, but considering Hamilton's present feelings toward me, I don't think I should rock the boat any more by screwing up the sentimental moment.

"Shit," Hamilton says, and grabs a lighter from the counter to reignite Nordica's candle. I think I would have just let this whole memory-to-treasure-forever moment go, but Hamilton is relentless. "Now, just as this center candle will keep our flame alive long after our candles have been extinguished, so too will we keep our memories alive long after our days at Fidelity High School draw to a close," she intones. "Now, everyone, blow out your candles."

We do, and once again, I'm wondering if Zelda didn't have some hand in all this. The whole thing smacks of Wiccan weirdo wannabe. We stand there stupidly in the near total darkness looking at the flame from the center candle. Our flame, but really, the flame of whoever got their candle there first.

"Okay, good night, everyone," Hamilton says.

"You should wish everyone sweet dreams," Zelda says, "because dreams are what help us to store our memories."

"Good night and sweet dreams," Hamilton says.

She walks us to the door like we're children. Maybe that's how she sees us. The October night is crisp and cool, laced with a taste of the winter that's just around the corner.

"Don't forget to blow out the candle," Nordica says.

"No," Hamilton says. "I'm not blowing this candle out. It's special. It needs to burn down on its own."

"Is that safe?" Olivia asks.

"Completely," Hamilton says.

But I can't help imagining how wonderfully ironic it would be if the candle we lit ends up burning down Hamilton's house. Maybe it would make more sense if I was the one who first reached the candle, the only one who lit the wick. Then it would be frighteningly appropriate. Metaphorically, it would be my flame destroying the house Hamilton built.

Nordica

On nights like this I don't mind not having a license, don't mind the walk home, which isn't a long one anyway. Olivia offered to drive me, but I wanted to walk. It gives me a chance to think, clear my head. Two more months and I can go for my driver's license, but I don't know if I will. I like having the excuse to head out on foot.

Hamilton's candle ceremony weighs on my mind. I know she wanted to do something symbolic to unify us all, but the candle thing felt forced. Traditions aren't something you can just make up. They have to build themselves over time. I could be wrong, but I don't think anyone was all that moved by the candle thing. Maybe Shelly, but it's hard to tell with her. She's such a fraud.

The other thing I think about—I can't help it, pessimism is an old friend—is the possibility that some crazy psychopath is lurking behind some bush, just waiting to jump out and slash my throat. Walking home down the dark, quiet street, I feel like the girl in a horror movie. The one everyone in the audience is always warning not to make all those stupid decisions, like, I don't know, refusing a ride with her friend just so she can walk alone through some dark and dangerous night.

But it's hard to get worked up about the dim possibility of a homicidal maniac lurking around the corner when the real world is so scary. High school. Popularity. Those are the things that nightmares are made of. Sure, I've woken up in a cold sweat after a dream about someone trying to kill me, but the thing is, with those dreams I can usually fall back to sleep because I realize that they are just dreams and there isn't really anything to be scared of. It's the dreams about wearing the wrong clothes or no clothes at all to school, or making some sort of horrible faux pas that turns the entire school against me, which really disturb me. When I wake up from one of those dreams, I spend the entire night tossing and turning because they've hit a little too close to home.

It's all fine and good for Hamilton and the rest of them to light their candles and talk about how the whole thing is almost over, but it isn't almost over, at least not for me. I've got two years of school to get through, and that seems like an eternity.

"Hey." The voice jumps out of the darkness and slashes my reverie. I'm so scared, I can't remember how to scream. I also seem to have lost the ability to move. Then the person that belongs to the voice steps into view. It's Alex. My heart is still beating too fast in my chest and adrenaline is coursing through my body.

"Alex," I manage, in a not-quite-steady voice. "I thought you went home hours ago." Then my keyed-up body starts wondering what Alex is doing out here in the middle of the night. Maybe Alex is actually a homicidal maniac. The thought is insane, but my brain insists on giving it serious consideration.

"Nordica. I did leave hours ago, but I just wasn't ready to go home. I've been enjoying the night, thinking."

"It's a good night for that," I agree.

"Let me walk you home," he says. "It's too late for you to be out here alone. You never know who you'll meet."

"Okay," I say, more to be polite than anything else. I know that my time for quiet contemplation has reached an end. I won't be doing anything except acting nervous and weird with a boy present, even if that boy happens to be Hamilton's boyfriend.

"I didn't see much of you tonight at the party," Alex says.

"I was there," I say.

"You better watch it. That's the sort of thing they'll engrave on your headstone."

The remark seems unnecessarily morbid, and I'm once again on the whole homicidal maniac track. You really can't know what's going on inside someone's head. Besides, Alex has always been a bit of an outsider, a bit of a loner.

"*She was there*," he says, waving his hands around

in such a way that I'm to understand he's envisioning the aforementioned headstone. "Sometimes I think you live too much in Hamilton's shadow. She's intimidating, believe me, I know, but you've got to be yourself. It's not good to keep yourself tucked away."

"In case you haven't noticed it, I'm not exactly a social butterfly," I say.

"Exactly, and I'm saying don't try so hard to be one when you're not. Just be yourself."

"If I was being myself, then I would never hang out with the other members of the clique. I would be, I don't know, playing oboe in the band or dissecting insects for extra credit in science club, or whatever it is that the socially inept do. If I was being myself, my life would be completely different."

"Bullshit." The word cuts through the night, and at first he doesn't say anything else. I wonder if the retort is to be his sole response. "So, I can't date Hamilton because I'm not of her ilk? That's the stupidest thing I ever heard. I said be yourself, Nordica, not be a stereotype."

He's right, of course, and I feel like an idiot. It's a bit like assuming he's some sort of psychopath just because he doesn't hang out with other high school boys and act like a general moron. It's completely unfair to assume there's something wrong with him just because he's smart enough to realize how trivial and pointless the whole high school thing is.

"Hey," Alex says. "Have you noticed Hamilton being

kind of down lately? I mean, about this being her last year of high school and all?"

"We had this candle-lighting ceremony tonight," I say, then immediately regret it. The candle ceremony was probably supposed to be a secret thing and here I've gone and blurted it out to Alex, who in turn will tell Hamilton, who will probably be pissed at me. "I don't know why she would be sad about school being over. She's going on to bigger and better things. I'm the one who'll be stuck here all on my own. Even you're leaving, Alex. You all are."

"Oh, don't count on that," Alex says. "Besides, you don't think that more than a few people might be envious of you, still having a year left before you have to go out there and face the great big ugly, scary world?"

I wonder what Alex means. Was he suggesting that he might not be graduating? Or was he suggesting that someone else might not be? I can't really tell, and I don't want to ask him because I'm sure that one way or another it will make me look like an idiot; of course, then I would be following Alex's directive to be myself.

"I wish I was done with high school," I say. "I've wished it was over almost as soon as it started."

"That's not how most of the popular girls talk."

"Don't stereotype me."

"Touché."

We have run out of sidewalk and reached my driveway.

"Home again, home again," Alex murmurs.

"Thanks," I say and mean it, and although I don't expect him to know it, don't want him to know it, I'm thanking him for the friendly conversation as much as for the walk. It's easily the longest conversation Alex and I have ever had, and for me, definitely the longest conversation with any member of the opposite sex. Our walk and our talk leave me with a warm feeling in my belly.

I'm halfway up my driveway when he calls out, "Don't ever change. Stay true to yourself."

"Right back at you," I answer, smoothly, coolly. This conversation thing isn't so hard to master. I should have tried it out sooner.

zelda

According to my horoscope, today's a four-star day and I'm going to have a thought-provoking conversation with someone who's a key player in my destiny. It's one of those days when I don't mind coming into school, because unlike other days, anything seems possible. Okay, I know that I probably shouldn't put so much stock in a syndicated astrology column, but there's something to the whole star-sign thing, as crazy as it may seem, and many days my horoscope seems to be more or less on target.

Of course, the first conversation of the day turns out to be less than thought-provoking. I see Olivia in the hallway on my way to first period and give her a more enthusiastic greeting than normal, on account of our candle-lighting ceremony a few nights ago. It really gave me new respect for Hamilton, that she would take the time to do something like that. And I know, for me, it really strengthened the bond that exists between us. We really are more than just friends; we're like sisters. I felt it that night, and I can feel it still.

Olivia takes my friendly greeting for an invitation to talk, which would be okay except I have history first period and Mr. James doesn't tolerate tardiness of any kind. I've had to make more than one trip to the office for a late pass at his insistence, and I'm not looking forward to another. In fact, I'm not sure what the quota is or whether or not I've reached it, but I have a strong suspicion that I'm about due for a detention, and I'm looking forward too much to my four-star day to have it spoiled. Well, there's always Hamilton and her seemingly magical ability to get me out of serving detention, but what if even her powers are not enough to save me?

"Sorry, Olivia," I say as I manage to maneuver by her. "I really can't talk right now."

She shouts something after me that sounds like, "Do you like soccer?" but that doesn't make a whole lot of sense. So I'm sure I misunderstood.

"What?" I shout back as I move swiftly down the hall, but I'm too far away, and she either doesn't hear me or doesn't feel like shouting an answer. As I jog the rest of the way to class, an unnecessary physical exertion it turns out, as I end up in my seat thirty seconds before the bell, I worry that this was my promised thought-provoking conversation. I'm pissed that I might have missed it all on account of a strict history teacher, but then it seems unlikely that Olivia would figure in my destiny.

The rest of the morning is uneventful, which makes me wonder if I was really reading the right horoscope. What if I read the wrong sign by mistake? What if the paper screwed up and ran tomorrow's horoscope today? It definitely doesn't seem like a four-star day. As if to prove that point, every single piece of lettuce in the salad bar is wilted at lunch time.

"Maybe I'll go see what they have for hot lunch," Nordica says as I stand there shuffling through the pieces of not-green lettuce with the stainless steel tongs.

"It's Taylor ham and cheese," I say.

"Oh," she says, and begins to arrange a few rubbery-looking cherry tomatoes on her plate.

When I finally get to our table, a few odd vegetables on my plate as if I'm on some bizarre Hollywood diet, Olivia is still talking about soccer and the strong bond I was feeling for these girls is already beginning to fade.

"Did anyone know that Fidelity has made it into the regional soccer playoffs?" Olivia asks. Hamilton makes a face that seems to indicate she suspects Olivia of being a pod person.

"Here's a better question," Shelly says. "Does anyone care that Fidelity has made it into the regional soccer playoffs?"

"Shelly, quit being a bitch," Hamilton says. "Though

seriously, Liv, why should we care about the soccer playoffs?"

"Well," Olivia says, "they're still a school team, and this is a big deal."

"Correction," Shelly says. "Football is a big deal. Soccer is a sport that nobody gives a shit about."

"Exactly," Olivia says. "All the more reason we should plan to be at the game to provide them with a cheering section."

"That's a good idea," Hamilton says.

"Please tell me you're joking," Shelly says.

"Hey, these are our friends and fellow students," Hamilton tells her. "We should be there to root for them. Besides, it will be fun. You know, I haven't gone to a single soccer game since I started high school."

"There's probably a very good reason for that," Shelly says. "As for them being our friends, I bet you couldn't name a single player on the soccer team."

"Of course I can," Hamilton says. "There's, ah . . . "

"Chance," Olivia supplies.

"That's right, Chance," Hamilton says. "Wasn't his gorilla costume a scream?"

"Is that who was in the gorilla suit?" I ask.

"Chance was Tarzan," Olivia says.

But then Shelly says, "Like it takes a lot of imagination to go to the costume shop and rent a gorilla suit. It's about as imaginative as soccer. Do you know how that game works? They just run up and down the field, back and forth, kicking some stupid ball around. They almost never score. It's as boring as coming to a Halloween costume in a gorilla suit."

I want to ask if anyone knows who was in the gorilla costume because I never did find out. Although I had forgotten all about that troubling feeling, something in me stirs a bit with the mention of the gorilla. The problem is that before I can ask, the talk has moved on to more about soccer and the game. Once again, I am left to wonder if this was my thought-provoking conversation.

The lunch conversation is so unimaginably boring that I leave early. The meager plate of vegetables gives me a good excuse, as I eat these up in less than five minutes.

On my way toward the school's back doors, the ones that read *Emergency Exit Only, Alarm Will Sound*, I run into Alex, who is busy hanging out in the hallway and looking cool. I can't help but think how much easier it is for Alex to look cool as Hamilton's boyfriend than it would be if he was only Alex Journer, without any royal connection.

"Are you . . . ?" he begins.

"Going outside in the middle of the day in violation of all school rules?" I supply. "Why, yes I am, but ask me if I give a shit."

"Actually, maybe I'll join you. I need some fresh air."

"Suit yourself."

Alex has always struck me as a bit too much of a hanger-on for my taste. I know you probably think that's a bit hypocritical coming from me, but it's different with

Alex. It's one thing to be someone's friend. It's another thing to be their boyfriend. I mean, if the man had any backbone whatsoever, he would just walk away, wouldn't he? Who cares that she's the most beautiful girl in the school? If you're nothing but her plaything, what's the point of the relationship, anyway? Alex likes for people to think that he's some sort of cool outsider, but the fact is, he's Hamilton's boyfriend, and as such is no better than any other spineless male.

We open the door and step outside, and of course, no alarm sounds (everyone who isn't a complete slave to idiotic rules knows that the security wires that are supposed to signal an alarm were severed long ago or never even connected). We step out onto the cement patio that runs along the back wall of the school and look out on the expanse of wasteland that is the school's property. It's really too chilly to be out there without jackets, but having walked boldly outside, I can't just turn tail and run back to the safety of the warm school.

"No lunch for you today?" Alex asks.

"All the lettuce was wilted," I say, even though he was probably looking for only a yes or no question. "Can I ask a question? It's personal."

"Fire away."

"Is she really spectacular in bed?"

"Hamilton?" he asks, with a little bit of a chuckle.

"Is there some other girl I should know about?"

"No, of course not. She's, well, yeah, I guess she is pretty spectacular."

"I don't want details," I say quickly, because I fear this is where he's going. "I just was wondering what a guy like you is doing with her, that's all."

"Are you sure she didn't put you up to this?"

"Unlike some people, I don't just do whatever Hamilton tells me to do."

"I'm not sure what you mean by that."

"She's got you wrapped around her finger, that's all. I don't get it."

"I love her, Zelda. I love her more than you can understand."

"Yeah, I guess so. It really is something I can't understand." I want to go inside. The cold is eating through my thin clothing.

"What about you, Zelda? You don't exactly seem like the type of girl that would be friends with Hamilton. So, why are you?"

I think he meant the question to somehow prove that it was ridiculous for me to ask why he was with Hamilton, but that's not what it does it all. It makes me think that it is pretty fucking weird how I insist on being Hamilton's friend when there's no reason on earth I should. Suddenly, that sisterly bond is gone and in its place is this vacuum. Why the hell am I friends with Hamilton?

"I don't know," I say, then I walk away, back inside. I look out the window at Alex. He's just standing there, looking out at the wasteland like he's thinking something very deep, and that's when it hits me. He's thinking about me. I have just had the promised profound conversation, and Alex is the one who plays a part in my destiny, by which I can only assume that Alex, with his dark, brooding eyes and his long, lean body, is my destiny. This seems like something that I should shy away from, but I don't. I've never felt quite so sure of anything before in my life.

Hamilton

Unlike Shelly Trust, most people were more than happy to come out and cheer on the soccer boys when I told them about our plan. Our home-team cheering section has filled up both sets of meager bleachers that easily hold the sum total of the soccer team's audience. A few of the cheerleaders have even showed up in uniform and made up some uninspired, soccer-specific cheers. Standing at the edge of the field and looking at what I was able to accomplish in only a few days gives me an immense sense of satisfaction.

Apparently the soccer team feels the same way. As they trot onto the field for their warm-up, there are shouts of surprise as they look over at the crowd.

"This is fantastic," Chance says to me as he takes the field. "This is way more than I had expected."

It's this sort of thing that I'll miss when school is over. Being able to make someone's day like that is such a great feeling. It's what I do, and I do it well.

I continue to hang out on the sidelines when the game begins, not because I'm admiring my handiwork or worried about not being able to find a seat in the crowded bleachers, but because I'm waiting for Alex, who seemed to indicate he would be here for the game. He hadn't been thrilled by the prospect when I told him about our plan. He's not very into sports, but when I told him it was about school spirit and solidarity, he seemed to understand. Though now I wonder if he's just figured he can avoid showing up. I'm sure he'll have some involved and implausible excuse for me later.

Shelly's absolutely right about soccer being a bit of a drag. It does seem to be a bunch of guys just running up and down the field. There are a few attempts at scoring, but since the goalies are allowed to use their hands as well as their feet, the ball never makes it into the goal. I know that it would be completely rude to walk away from the game, even for a few minutes, especially after promising everyone else that it would be a fun and exciting afternoon, but I also know I could probably leave for a half hour and not miss much at all. I don't even need to go that far, just find out if Alex is on the premises and, if so, drag him back to the soccer field with me where he belongs.

The temptation is really great, but then Chance gives

me a wave as he runs past in pursuit of the ball, and as I reluctantly wave back, I realize I can't walk away. Everyone would see me leave, including the players, and they need my support. They also need to score a goal already, before everyone falls asleep.

OLIVIA

Despite all of Shelly's mock yawns and complaints, the game was an exciting one, and while admittedly I missed much of the action on the field as my eyes were glued to one player, it was a close game, and unfortunately for Fidelity and Chance, the final score was three to two, with St. Paul's winning. In any event, a certain sexy, sweaty team captain is crestfallen and in need of some moral support.

"You played a great game," I say as I fall into step with him up the path back to the school.

"Not quite good enough, apparently," he says.

"It was a tough break," I say. "It really could have gone either way."

"Yeah, I know what you mean. I really thought we had them until Popes scored that last goal. He just came out of nowhere with that one. We really did play our best today, and I think we have you and all your friends to thank. That was awesome."

I don't tell him that he probably had Hamilton to thank. I didn't know most of the people there. They were her friends, or her wannabe friends at least.

I don't know where the mighty one has gone off to, but I see her boyfriend sitting on a bench up ahead and remember, too late, his weird grudge against Chance.

"Hey, Alex," I say, in a voice more friendly than my normal one.

He doesn't respond, only scowls and gives a curt nod. He's such a moody bastard. Chance's face, already flushed from all that running around, seems to turn a shade or two pinker. I wonder what the hell happened between these two. I want to ask Chance, but decide against it. Maybe later, when I get to know him better, I could ask. For now, I'll avoid bringing up anything unpleasant.

"I really appreciate everything you've done for me," Chance says when we're out of Alex's earshot and almost up to the school. I'm wondering where the hell he's going with this, and then I see her, sitting on the grass just ahead. Donna Lukowski, that skanky bitch, is looking in our direction and smirking at me. I mouth the word "whore" at her, but I sincerely doubt her lip-reading ability is much better than her regular reading ability. Realizing that his I-appreciate-everything speech is his way of sending me on my merry way so that he can run right into Donna's waiting arms, I start to back up.

"I've got to go," I say, nodding back in the direction we've just come from.

"Right," he says. "I understand."

"And it looks like you've got another adoring fan."

He turns to look and Donna begins waving, in case he didn't notice all the flesh that's out on display.

"Well, thanks again," he says to me. "You have no idea how much this meant to me."

I don't stay and watch the two of them. I feel slimy. The son of a bitch used me. He played up to me to get his precious cheering section, and now that the season's over, it's so long, Olivia. Thanks for all you've done for me, now fuck off.

I walk back over to Alex, who's still busy scowling and being moody.

"Why do you hate Chance so much?" I ask. He looks up at me, and there are (I'm not joking) tears welled up in his eyes. He really is worse than a girl.

"Why?" he repeats, in a voice soggy with tears.

"Yeah."

"Why do you think?" he asks.

"If I knew, I wouldn't be asking, would I?"

"You wouldn't understand," he says.

"Try me. I think maybe I would."

He looks up at me then, with puppy dog eyes. He's pathetic, but I suppose that's what Hamilton sees in him. He's the kind of guy she can bend to her will without much work at all.

"I don't like that you have a crush on him."

"I realize that, but what have you got against him?"

He takes a deep breath, and I'm waiting for him to tell me some long, involved story that will illustrate Chance's scumbag nature, but instead he says in a very quiet voice, "I'm in love with you."

"What?"

There is no time for me to respond further because Alex stands up, takes my face in his hands, and kisses me, right there in the open. It's shocking and amazing, and any other time I would have just pushed him away, but I know Chance the dick is still standing there just outside the school, and I hope to hell he's watching as I kiss Alex back.

Shelly

"I don't know," Debbie says, stretching her foot out in front of her and examining the sneaker from every possible angle. "I mean, it's pink, and it does have the kind of sole I like, but I'm just not sure. Do you think, well, I mean, it's almost like it makes my foot look big, right? Am I imagining it?"

It takes all my power to stop my eyes from rolling involuntarily, as I now am forced to pretend to study Debbie's foot in the stupid fucking sneaker. I've spent three hours of my life, which I will never get back, traipsing all over the mall to find Debbie Shune the perfect sneaker. It had to be pink, leather not canvas, low top, with the tannish-colored rubber sole that she likes so much, and now we've finally found it, and just when I thought our quest was over, she's decided that no, this isn't the right shoe because it makes her foot look too big. Give me a fucking break.

Caitlin is no help either. She's just egged Debbie on the whole time, and now, God help us, she's examining Debbie's foot, scrunching up her face, and nodding. I know that if I don't dive in now, Caitlin could open her mouth and utter something that will keep us here at the mall until our hair turns gray and our tits start to sag to our waist.

"It's just because of the angle you're looking at it from," I say. "You can't look at shoes while holding your feet up in the air. You've got to stand up and walk around and look down at your feet. When you hold your feet at a funny angle like that, they always look huge." Especially, I think, if you have size 9 ½ feet.

Debbie complies with my suggestion and starts walking around the shoe store, and I know there is a God in heaven because a smile comes over her face. Hallelujah, this shopping trip is going to end before we're old enough to collect social security.

"They look awesome," Caitlin says. I take back every bad thought I've ever had about Caitlin. Well, okay, at least half of them.

"Yeah, they do, but you know, maybe I should have brought my sweater with me," Debbie says. "I'm not sure that they're the right pink. I'm worried they might clash."

"There's a rule in fashion. I read it in a magazine," I lie, "that you can always mix and match different shades of pink. Pinks never clash. That's what makes it such a great color."

"God, I'm so glad you came shopping with us," Debbie gushes. Oh please, spare me. "I don't know what we would have done without you."

They probably would have been wandering around the mall until closing trying to find the perfect pair of sneakers, and I would have been enjoying my leisure time, but that's neither here nor there because I'm not here for the fun of it. I am here because building alliances is an important part of becoming popular. If I want to be the most popular girl in the school, then I need to build an entire network of alliances. It's unfortunate that I am forced to start with such a vacuous pair of ninnies, but sometimes you have to play the hand you are given.

"I think we should celebrate with smoothies at the food court," Caitlin says, when we've finally left the store with what you would think was the sneaker equivalent of the holy grail.

"Smoothies it is," I say in my best celebratory voice. "My treat."

We're sucking down our smoothies when across the way we notice Chance and some other soccer dweeb, along with Donna the drunk. Chance spots us and gives us a smile and a wave, but Donna, who hasn't quite boozed away all her brain cells, wisely steers him away.

"I heard she's in AA," Caitlin says.

"Her parents want to send her away to rehab," Debbie chimes in.

"Well, whatever she's up to, she's definitely packing on the pounds. Did you see those jeans? I'm not quite sure how she crammed her ass into them."

This has Caitlin and Debbie laughing so hard that Debbie starts snorting strawberry banana smoothie right out her nose. Ah, yes, the joys of spending Saturday afternoon at the mall with two of the biggest airheads in the senior class. People have no idea just how much work goes into becoming popular.

It's six at night by the time I finally drop Caitlin and Debbie off at their respective houses. I'm completely exhausted and have a gigantic headache. The problem is, I'm nowhere near my goal, and I don't know how much more of this I can take. I know there's got to be an easier way, and I have to figure it out soon.

Maybe instead of wasting my time with flighty girls, I should be going after some popular member of the opposite sex. At least with a guy, I wouldn't have to waste my Saturday wandering around the mall, shoe shopping. Hell, for guys, the ideal girl is one that gives them plenty of time and freedom to do their own thing but is there for a quick screw when the urge strikes them. It sure as hell beats trying to find the perfect pair of pink sneakers.

The problem is, there aren't too many available popular guys. The thing with being popular is, you can usually have all the ladies you want. I would have to start with a smaller fish, some guy who's second-tier popular at best.

My first thought is Chance. He was on the guest list, and now that we've decided that soccer is a real sport (even though I strongly disagree), he qualifies as a jock. Sure, he's technically with Donna, but after the whole peeing-in-her-pants episode, he has to be suffering from a case of wandering eye, and let's face it, he can do a lot better than Donna. He isn't that bad looking, either. Not exactly what one could call hot, but still decent enough. Bedding him wouldn't be too hard, and I'm almost sure it would be a big boost to my own standings in the unofficial race for queen of the school.

I'm already working out a plan for something I'm officially thinking of as "Operation Chance" when, as I drive through town, I notice a lone figure sitting at the coffee shop's sidewalk table even though it's barely fifty degrees outside, staring moodily into space. If I'm going to try to snag a guy who already has a girlfriend, why start as far down on the pecking order as Chance? If I'm going to go through all that work, shouldn't I start higher, and if I'm going to start higher, why not start at the absolute top?

Of course, it's absolutely and completely insane. I can't just steal Hamilton's boyfriend. For starters, if it doesn't work, it could backfire in a big-time way and things could get very ugly for yours truly. On the other hand, that's just a pessimistic way of looking at it. It's not like I want Alex to fall in love with me anyway. Yuck! I just need him to betray Hamilton. Because when he does that, I will, in one brilliant move, diminish Hamilton's standing while elevating my own. It's all so beautiful that I know, hell or high water, I will find a way to make it succeed. Alex won't know what hit him.

The biggest problem will be seducing someone as completely weird as Alex, but underneath it all, he's still a guy, right? How hard can it be? No pun intended.

Nordica

Exhibit A is called *Blonds Have More Fun*. It's two cheerleaders. I should know their names—Stacy, I think, is the one, and the other has some other appropriate and completely forgettable name. They've just whispered some bits of juicy gossip back and forth to each other in the crowded hallway and are now laughing over whatever the story is. Their grins are enormous. I snapped it last Tuesday during fourth period. I thought, at the time, that they looked ridiculous, and I thought that the camera would capture that, would make a mockery of them. But instead, all that the lens captured is their utter elation. They are truly happy, and this is what the camera has shown me; not their idiocy, but their joy. How does one become this happy, I want to know? Can I ever become this happy?

"Hey, sweetie," my mom says. She pokes her head into

my room. She's in her uniform, ready to go to work. There's a pitying sort of smile on her face as she glances down at the scrapbook, like even she knows I'm pathetic. "Is everything all right?" she asks.

"I'm fine," I say.

"There's some leftover ziti you can toss in the microwave for dinner," she says.

"I'm not helpless. I can make my own dinner."

"My little girl is all grown up." She gets a wistful sort of look in her eye. Then she steps into my room to plant a kiss on top of my head. "My little Janey." I stiffen at the baby name, but she shows no sign of noticing. "Have a good night. No wild parties." I smile at that last part, as if I'm capable of throwing a wild party.

I wait until I hear her head down the hall, then paste the picture of the smiling blonds into my scrapbook in the next available spot, beneath a picture of Alex I took one day after school. He's sitting on a bench gazing off into the distance, his expression sad and contemplative, a complete contrast to the giggling cheerleaders. It's a great picture of him—the dreamy look in his eyes, the set of his jaw. I suppose I've never spent much time looking at Alex, and he does sort of go out of his way to dress and act so oddly that you tend to not realize that beneath all the Alexness there's this very attractive young man. I mean, I understand, I think, what it is Hamilton sees.

I've been thinking about Alex a lot lately. Not like that. I just mean I've been thinking about what he said to me that night after Hamilton's Halloween party, about being myself and just having a good time instead of worrying about what people think. It's good advice, but it's not easy to follow.

I find myself tracing the silhouette of his face with my finger, smudging the glossy surface of the photograph with my skin oils. Petting his hair as if he were a stuffed animal rather than a two-dimensional image of a person. Before I can stop myself, I pick up the phone and dial his number. When he picks up, I almost hang up, but instead I'm silent.

"Hello? Hello?" Alex says. "Hello? Anyone there?"

"Alex, it's Nordica. I was wondering if I could talk to you."

"Sure," he says. "What's up?" I look down at his picture, the dreamy eyes. He looks so noble, so far removed from the tawdry world of high school.

"In person," I say, "not over the phone. I hate talking on the phone."

"Did you want to meet me somewhere? Do you like coffee?"

"I don't have my license yet."

"I could pick you up."

Alex drives a convertible. Don't ask me what kind; I don't know anything about cars. It's white, and the vinyl top is black, which is up tonight because it's cold with a chance of flurries.

I must look as scared as I feel, because when I sit down in the passenger seat Alex says, "Nordica? What's wrong?"

"Is it hard being alone all the time?"

"I'm not alone right now."

"I mean how you don't really have any friends, how you don't hang out with people at school."

"I'm not really a people person. There's only a handful of people I can tolerate."

"I've been thinking a lot about what you said, about just letting go, just being me, and I don't think I can as long as I'm part of the clique."

"Of course you can."

"No. I can't. In order to be myself, I would have to break free from them."

"I don't think it's that easy."

"It's impossible," I agree. I look over at him. He's watching the road, his eyes more alert than his dreamy eyes in the picture. I wonder if I'm one of the handful of people he can tolerate.

He pulls off the road. We aren't anywhere—not at the coffee shop or even a parking lot, just on the shoulder of the road. He looks over at me, and he looks sad. He pities me. I can see it in his eyes. It makes me feel resentful.

"Why do you think that I have the answers?" he asks.

"You're alone most of the time," I say. "I just want to know what that feels like, what it feels like to be alone."

Then Alex starts to cry. Not bawling his eyes out or anything, but there are a few tears streaking down his cheeks and I wish I had my camera. I want to capture a close-up image of this tear as it rolls slowly down his cheek, but I couldn't do that even if I did have my camera, because Alex is hurting. All this time, I thought he'd been a loner by choice, but now I see maybe this isn't so, maybe he wants to have friends, people he can tolerate. Maybe he's sad to be alone.

I don't know why, but I reach out and brush away that tear rolling down his cheek, and he grabs my hand. I try to pull it back, but he doesn't relinquish it, just clutches it in his own, holds it to his face. Then he rests his head on my shoulder and wipes his tear-dampened face on the sleeve of my jacket.

"Is it sad to be alone?" I ask. "I'm sorry I made you cry."

"No," he says. "It's not your fault. It's not your fault."

zelda

I'm walking through the hallway on my way to the next-to-last class of the day when soccer star Chance claps me on the back, shouts "Woohoo!" and goes running down the hallway. The event would have puzzled me for hours if, not thirty seconds later, Shelly hadn't grabbed hold of me and started dragging me down the hallway.

"Release my arm, now," I say.

"Have you seen it?" Shelly says. "It's a travesty." She drags me into the nearest girls' room and slams the door closed with her ass.

"Let go of my arm, now." She releases me reluctantly, and I rub the spot where her fake nails had dug into my skin, right through the sleeve of my shirt. "What's a travesty?"

"The guest list. She's gone completely off her noggin."

"Who?" I say, still thinking about the bizarre encounter with Chance.

"Hamilton! Who else?"

"Was Chance what's-his-face on it?" I ask.

"Yes. Why? Is there something going on between you two?"

"No. He just seemed insanely happy."

"Yeah, well, he's one of the few people on the list who makes any sense at all. The rest of them, well, you should see the list, it's bizarre and she left all sorts of people off. Caitlin and Debbie didn't make it, and I think even you would admit they're two of the most popular girls in the senior class."

"Isn't Debbie the girl with the ridiculous pink sneakers?"

"They're called *stylish*, Zelda. I know you don't realize this, but clothing comes in colors other than black."

"So, when is this party?" I ask.

"Thanksgiving weekend, which if you ask me is a stupid time for a party. People go away to visit relatives. They're not going to be around to attend some party, and when they get a look at some of the people who are on the guest list, they're not going to want to attend the party. There's even one of your kind of freaks on the list."

"Am I supposed to know what that means?"

"Some girl who wears too much eyeliner and writes poetry and shit. I mean, what the hell?"

Somebody starts to come into the bathroom, but Shelly slams the door shut and holds it there.

"Shelly, this is all terribly fascinating, but I've got a class to get to."

"Somebody really needs to talk to her about this."

"It's Hamilton's party. She can invite whoever the hell she wants."

Shelly is bigger and stronger than me, but somehow I manage to shove her out of the way long enough to get the door open. I step out, right into some goth girl with too much eye makeup.

"Hey, see you at the party," the girl says in a completely sincere voice. Okay, Shelly has a point. That was a little bit freaky.

I wonder if Hamilton put that girl on the guest list because of me. Was it supposed to appease me in some way? Was it supposed to convince me she really does care about and support me? Was it supposed to steer me clear of the thoughts that have lately crept into my head concerning Alex Journer, the man who is, I am positive now, my destiny?

I haven't said anything to Alex about what I've figured out; I've barely spoken to him since that day we spent the last few minutes of lunch period outside in the cold, having our thought-provoking conversation. I doubt he would understand anyway.

It isn't like I can come out and tell him I think we're fated to be together. He'd think I was crazy. Hamilton is his girlfriend. I'm just one of her trusty sidekicks, a short, dark-haired, stranger version of the queen of the school. A pale imitation of the girl he's in love with. What could he ever see in me? I don't yet have the answer to that question, and until I do, I'm afraid to make a move. Besides, I'm not sure how these things work, but I think maybe I should just wait for fate to work its magic.

Now, though, I wonder if I've somehow telegraphed my feelings to Hamilton herself. Why else would she put this strange, freaky girl on the guest list? It seems a move calculated to appease me in some way, and I don't know why. But if she thinks putting some stupid girl who I don't even know on her guest list is going to stop me from stealing her boyfriend, she's in for a big surprise.

Hamilton

"You're awfully quiet," I say to Alex. He's shirtless, stretched out on my bed, his hair a mess, but in that cute, sexy kind of way.

The first snow day of the year has given us an extra-long Thanksgiving break. I won't see Alex tomorrow because he's spending the day with relatives out of state, so I invited him over, but he's being his usual moody self.

"You ready for your party?" he asks.

"You'll be back by Saturday night. You promised."

"I'll be there," he says.

I don't know how it happened, but a gulf has grown between the two of us. It's not like we're fighting or anything, but we're not as close as we were just a month or so ago. It's not just Alex. I feel it with the clique as well, which means it must have something to do with me. Or more likely, as I suspect, everyone else is already looking ahead, already starting to move on to their future lives. I'm the only one who's still one hundred percent here, the only one who isn't yet ready to say goodbye.

"Are you here right now?" I ask.

"What?"

"You heard me. How do I know if you're really here? You seem so far away."

"How do you know if I'm really here?" He laughs. "Right. I'm always here, Hamilton, always, even when you're not."

The remark stings. I don't let it show. That's what he wants. He's looking at me, waiting for me to open up to him. Sometimes I do, but I usually feel like I am saying the same things over and over again.

"Did you get a chance to look at the guest list?" I ask.

"I never look at it, Hamilton. You should know that by now."

"It's unusual, the list."

Unusual is an understatement. The list is a completely random sampling of people. A lot of the regulars are on it. They'd have to be, or else it would look too suspicious, but other than that, there's no rhyme or reason to the names that appear there, almost as if someone flipped through a yearbook and randomly chose names. Maybe they did.

I didn't write that list. I don't know who did. I'm assuming it was a member of the clique—I don't know who else would be that brazen. But I'm not sure who it was, and I haven't spent too much time trying to figure out why because I'm scared of what the answer might be. The intent seems malicious, and that's disturbing.

"What are you thinking right now?" I ask.

He looks at me with those big dark eyes, the ones that can make me melt inside. He's so gorgeous, and I know that I love him too much.

"I'm thinking you're the most beautiful girl I've ever met," he says. "I'm thinking how much I love you, and I'm thinking how sometimes I don't even know who you are."

"You know me better than anyone, Alex."

"I know," he says.

I close my eyes and rest my head on his chest. He strokes my hair as if I were a little girl, and I wish I was. I wish I was a little girl. I wish I never had to grow up.

OLIVIA

Alex calls me a few hours before Hamilton's party. I've avoided him since the day of the kiss, but he's called several times since then, and sometimes I've actually talked to him. I don't want to talk to him today, but I pick up the phone thinking it's Hamilton or one of the clique.

"Olivia?" His voice is quiet, almost as if he's whispering, as if he thinks Hamilton will hear our conversation if he talks too loud.

"Alex. Hey. Did you have a nice Thanksgiving?"

"I need to see you."

"I'll be at the party tonight."

"No, I need to see you now. Please."

"Hamilton's my best friend."

"She's my girlfriend. I love her."

"Then why do you keep calling here?"

"I know you made that guest list."

I click off the phone, dropping it from my hand as if it were on fire. How does Alex know that I posted that guest list? Does anyone else know?

I sit on my bed, hugging my knees to my chest. Ironically, I wish Hamilton were here so that I could have someone to talk to about all this, but of course, Hamilton is the last person I can talk to about this.

It seems almost certain that it was Hamilton who figured out that the guest list was my doing, and she likely was the one who told Alex. He isn't someone who would care about the guest list. Alex is above such things. So I can rest assured that Alex won't tell anyone else, and, of course, Hamilton can't tell anyone else. She has to pretend like the whole thing is her doing, that she's still captain of this ship.

Still, I hadn't counted on Hamilton finding out it was me. I was stupid. I didn't think it would be so obvious. And it wouldn't be, to anyone else, but Hamilton has known me too long. That list was brimming with clues that must have pointed directly at me. I'm an idiot.

She probably sees me as a rebellious child, one who's proving her independence with some stupid stunt, and really, that's all it is. I'm deluded if I think posting a phony guest list is going to have any far-reaching consequences for the students of Fidelity High. A few popular kids won't be at the party, oh boo hoo, and a few kids who never had a chance in hell of being popular will get a chance to see how the other half lives. I'm like a high school Robin

Hood, only instead of money, the commodity in question is good old popularity. It sounds so noble, but take a look at the list and you'll probably spy more than one purely personal decision. Like, say, the fact that Chance is once again on the guest list, while Donna is not.

Outside, a car door slams. A few seconds later an angry fist begins to pound out an incessant rhythm on the back door. I peak out the window and see Alex's car in the driveway. I could just stay up here in my bedroom. At some point he'll give up and leave. It's a tempting option, but I know I need to go down there. We need to have this all out. I can't avoid him forever.

I take my time going downstairs, and open the door as calmly as if I was just stepping outside to check the weather. Alex is flushed. His eyes look wild, and when he walks inside he does so at a near run.

"Olivia," he says, and in his emotional state his voice comes out like a shout.

"You need to calm down. My mother's upstairs getting ready." He cocks his head, listening to the sound of the shower running. It seems to make him come to his senses. He calms down a bit.

"I need to see you," he says.

"Well, I'm right here."

"Are you?" He begins pacing the small kitchen. "Look, I don't care about the guest list."

"I know that."

"I'm not even going to ask you why you did it. I've got

a pretty good idea why, but it doesn't matter. I don't really care about all that stuff. All I care about is you."

"Alex, there can't be anything between us."

"Give me one good reason, and Hamilton doesn't count."

"Okay, then how about the fact that I'm not interested in you."

"Liar!" he shouts.

"Oh, please, just because Hamilton Best is dating you does not make you God's gift to women. Hamilton's got weird taste."

"You're going to tell me you didn't feel it, that day after the soccer game?"

"Alex." I stop myself, because I am about to say that I only let him kiss me because I wanted to make Chance jealous. It's the truth, but it sounds so incredibly shallow. It sounds like something Shelly would do, and I don't want Alex to think I'd stoop to that level even if I had. "I was pretty confused."

"No you weren't. You were following your instincts."

"Alex, I like Chance. A lot."

"Chance!" His voice cracks on the word. He slams his fist down on the counter top hard. He bites his lip either from the pain or from rage, or maybe a little of both. "Why? What does he have that I don't have? What makes him so great?"

"I don't know," I say. "I just like him. I'm attracted to him, but I know I can't have him."

"You do?"

"He's dating Donna, and you're dating Hamilton. So I guess that means I'm on my own."

"No, Olivia, you're anything but on your own. What if I told you that you mean more to me than Hamilton?"

"I'd say you were a complete dick. Hamilton's my friend."

"Is she?"

I'd underestimated him. Perhaps he'd figured out the guest list thing all on his own. Maybe Alex isn't as out of touch as he pretends to be. Maybe all those times I thought he was off in his own little world, he was really paying keen attention to the wonderfully thrilling world of high school politics. Or maybe he's just talking out of his ass.

"I've got a party to get ready for," I say.

"Tell me you're not interested in me and I'll forget anything even happened."

"Nothing happened, Alex."

"Just tell me, Olivia."

"I already told you how I feel," I say.

"Tell me you're not interested in me."

I'm not interested in him. Am I? A couple of minutes ago, the whole thing seemed so cut and dry: Alex is Hamilton's boyfriend, I like Chance, Chance likes Donna, therefore I will spend my senior year devoted to my studies, with a little extracurricular idol-toppling thrown in for good measure.

"Tell me you're in love with Hamilton and I'll stop at nothing to make sure her senior year is completely flawless," I say.

"What?" All the pacing, all the emotion, drains out of Alex in a single moment of genuine surprise.

"Why don't you tell me why you're really here?" I say.

"I'm in love with you."

"No. You just stopped being in love with Hamilton."

Shelly

The emotional and irrational part of me wanted to skip out on this party. But clearly this would be a form of social suicide I can ill afford, for despite the alarming number of unfit persons who have somehow made it onto the guest list, this will still rank as one of the biggest social events of the year. To not attend would be utterly disastrous. Moreover, I have decided to take the optimistic view that being surrounded by so many non-entities will only cause others to see just how exceptional I am. There was a time when I would have worried about the tarnishing effects of being around so many losers, but I've lately taken a broader view of things. Still, I don't have to be happy about attending this party.

"Shelly, lend a hand with the refreshments," Olivia says. She's never heard about honey and its attractive properties vis-à-vis flies; not, of course, that I'm comparing myself to an insect. It's just a simile or a metaphor or one of those goddamn things.

"I can't," I say. "People will be arriving soon."

"Exactly. We need to get stuff set up."

"I need to be here by the door when they arrive." To prove this, I wave my handwritten copy of the guest list at her.

"What the hell is that?"

"The guest list. Do I need to remind you about what happened last time? Somebody needs to guard against crashers. Though I can't imagine why anyone would want to crash."

"You can't just turn people away because you don't like their shoes or whatever."

"The list," I say, waving it again for her benefit. "The list is absurd, but it's still gold, and if they're on here, they'll be getting in."

"I can't believe you're going to sit there and check names."

I usually end up doing a hefty amount of the grunt work because the apathy of the others interferes with their ability to perform such chores. Any of the rest of them would readily admit that checking off names is a good idea, but none of them would actually bother to do it. They fail to realize how important it is to pay attention to the details, and this being a solid middle-class town, nobody understands that it's follow-through that wins tennis matches.

I suspect this whole business of checking the guest list will weed out at least one undesirable who will attempt to sneak their way in. There was definitely an extra attendee at the Halloween party, and such a situation can be entirely prevented with the sacrifice I'm so willing to make.

Also, it will give me a chance to converse with what is likely to be the first guest through the door, a Mr. Journer, and I've spent the better part of my afternoon figuring out just what topics our friendly banter will cover. Having drawn upon my store of knowledge in how to flirtatiously speak with men, I'm pretty sure that it will not be long before unsophisticated Alex finds himself absolutely smitten and unable to resist my charms.

"Shelly, I don't recall giving you permission to set up a guest list checkpoint at my party," Hamilton says.

"I'm providing a service that will be of benefit to everyone who attends tonight."

"How? By annoying them before they even get a chance to take off their coat? Absolutely not."

"I realize that in the past we've not done such things, but sometimes we need to reevaluate our methods and make positive changes."

"What a load of bullshit," Hamilton says. "I see a future for you as a politician, but in the meantime, why don't you help us in setting up the refreshments. There will be no door detail tonight."

"But Hamilton, you don't realize how important this is?"

"Correction. I realize that it's not at all important."

I know that protesting further will be of no use; when

Hamilton gets her mind set on something, there's no swaying it. Besides, I feel pretty confident that I can simply perform my check once the party is underway. It'll be completely inefficient, but since there can be no check at the door, I'll have to settle for this. It does throw a huge monkey wrench into my well-planned-out conversation with Alex, so I'll have to see if I can't somehow corner him once things are underway and rework my prepared banter to meet the occasion. Well, I hadn't expected it to be a great night, and now it's getting worse.

"Shelly," Hamilton says, holding out her hand. I give her a blank look, as I am completely mystified as to what she could possibly want from me. "The list."

"It's not your original. I copied this out myself, by hand."

"Fork it over."

"I don't see what you could possibly need it for."

"I'm not going to have you walking around all night checking names off the list. This isn't a census. It's a party."

"Hamilton, there was an extra person at the Halloween party. You don't want that to happen again, do you?"

"What I recall about the Halloween party was that you insisted on spending the night counting heads and reporting to me, on more than one occasion, your suspicion that there was someone at the party that didn't belong here. It was tiresome and pointless."

"And it could all be prevented if you let me check everyone in at the door."

"Just hand me the list. Now."

I reluctantly comply. This is why it's so frustrating to

be Hamilton's friend. Here's an instance where I see a situation and a way to fix things, and Hamilton refuses to listen. Ordinarily, I would just rely on my memory to do a mental check-in of party attendees, but with some of the freakier folk on the list, I don't even know who the hell they are. How can I make her wake up and see the damage she's inflicting on herself? I don't know, but before long she'll see the mistake she's made when she realizes that I've jumped ahead of her in terms of popularity standings and showed her up as a failure at the game she thinks she plays so well.

Nordica

If I was being myself, I wouldn't be at this party. The real Nordica Freemingle can think of at least a dozen things she'd rather be doing, but the real Nordica Freemingle doesn't have the guts to do what she wants to do. So she's stuck here, while some annoying guy in her class who should have never made the guest list flirts shamelessly with her.

"So, I really have to say," Bill says, "I'm so happy to be here." It's the fifth or sixth time he's uttered some version of this sentiment, I've lost track. He's already told me all about how being able to go to this party meant so much to him that he curtailed a weekend with his grandparents just to be here, and that he never thought he'd have the opportunity to attend a real live Hamilton party. The real me wholeheartedly agrees with this, but being voiceless was forced to hold back any and all snarky but appropriate comments.

By the time Bill gets into telling me his concerns about buying his mom the perfect Christmas gift (he bought her a sweater last year that she really loved, but he doesn't want to get a sweater again this year and jewelry and perfume are out because she seldom wears those), I'm scanning the room for someone, anyone, who can save me from this hell.

It's Alex who spots my distress, sidles up to me, and throws a chummy arm over my shoulder that sends Bill scurrying off to bore some other defenseless creature to tears.

"Alex, thank you. I didn't think I'd ever get away from him."

"You wouldn't have," he says. "At least not by standing still. I thought we talked about this."

"Circumstances are against me," I say.

"You're making excuses. You really need to enjoy yourself and have fun."

"That's not something I can do if I'm trapped at this party."

"Good point," Alex says. "Should we leave?"

I smile at that, and Alex smiles back. Even though I know he's kidding, a part of me kind of wishes he wasn't. "I don't think I can leave," I say.

"No, I suppose I'm stuck here as well."

"Well, on the bright side, there's a lot of new faces here."

"And a lot of unusual faces."

"Do you think Hamilton did that on purpose? I mean, because of Thanksgiving and all."

It's been driving me crazy since she posted the guest list. It just doesn't make any sense why all sorts of weird people were on there. She must have had some reason for doing it, but she isn't telling any of us.

"Maybe," Alex says. "She doesn't really talk with me about that sort of stuff."

"What do you talk about, then?"

"Not a whole lot, anymore."

"Oh." I hate when I ask a question and get an answer that isn't what I expected, especially when the answer reveals information I don't know how to react to. What does he mean, he and Hamilton don't talk about much anymore? Does that mean they're fighting? Does it mean they have nothing in common? Why is he telling me this? How am I supposed to react? How am I supposed to feel?

"It's crazy, but before long the school year will be half over," I say, but my attempt to steer the conversation in another direction doesn't quite work.

"Yeah, she's really freaked out about the end of high school," Alex says. "I'm kind of ready to move on, but I understand how she feels. It's hard for her."

"Nothing's ever hard for Hamilton."

"You overestimate her."

What can I say? Isn't it just like a guy to see a girl as all vulnerable and in need of protection? If I didn't know better, I'd say that Hamilton is some sort of superhero disguised as a high school student. She certainly doesn't know the first thing about overcoming a challenge. For her there are no roadblocks, no hurdles. She truly leads a charmed life.

"She's going to keep on being Hamilton no matter where she is," I say. "It doesn't matter if she's in high school or college or off in the farthest corners of the world. She'll just do what she's always done, somewhere else."

"Without the clique, she won't be who she is, and she thinks she's going to lose all of you after high school."

"Well, of course she will. I've got another year to go, and I can't imagine any of the others are going to keep following her around. They've got their own lives to lead."

"That's what she's scared of," Alex says, and whether it's true or not, I can tell he definitely believes it. It's interesting to think that Hamilton is scared of losing us. My guess is she's just scared of having to start over from scratch. Which is interesting, since that's exactly what I'm scared of. It's also what I want most in the world, and that's the difference between us. Hamilton's fear is one of dread. Mine is one of anticipation.

zelda

The party is nothing but one giant "I told you so." All this time, I've thought Hamilton's guest lists were completely superficial and based strictly on who she considered popular enough to make the cut. I now see the party-planning genius that she is—that all this time, her hand-selected lists have been based on some secret formula she's figured out for achieving maximum party potential. I always took Hamilton only inviting certain types of people as a sort of slap in the face, but it turns out she might have had a good reason for doing things her way.

So while it seems like a good idea, the all-inclusive party, the party with a well-rounded mix of the student body, now I see just why Hamilton refused to listen to me before. A good forty-five minutes into the party, everyone is still standing around awkwardly, whispering amongst themselves in little groups and looking around nervously at all the other little groups. The attendees look more like displaced refugees than they do like teenagers having a good time on a Saturday night. The party is weird, and even though I normally like weird, even I have to admit it's the lamest Hamilton party I've ever attended.

"Hey, great party," says Chance, shoving a handful of chips in his mouth.

"Hah," I say. "It sucks."

Standing together, we form another pair of huddled refugees in the sea of isolated groups.

"Maybe everyone ate too much turkey. It can make you sleepy."

"Stop making excuses. It's a crappy party. I hate to admit it, but this is what happens when too many unpopular kids are on the guest list. There's a reason they're not popular, after all. They're boring."

"Well, it's just one party, and Donna doesn't even really care about not being on the list. She had to go up to New England to visit some relatives anyway."

I nod to be kind, but I have no idea who Donna is. Apparently I'm supposed to know. Shelly would know, but I don't know where she is. The last I saw her, she appeared to be making the rounds, talking to everyone she could, even people she considered non-entities. Maybe she's turning over a new leaf.

"Hey, so I thought it was great how everyone came to the playoff game. You know, you really didn't have to do that. It meant a lot to me."

"Well, it's good to have school spirit for all our sports.

We talked about getting a group together to cheer for the cross-country team, but there was a scheduling conflict."

I don't know why I am doing this, talking out my ass like this. I'm not even sure if Fidelity has a cross-country team. Furthermore, I don't know why Chance is standing here talking to me. Well, probably because he doesn't know any of these loser kids in their little whispering groups, but still, other than the fact that he plays soccer, I don't know enough about him to make any sort of intelligent small talk. Where the hell is Shelly when you need her?

"You know what this party needs?" Chance says.

"To come to an end," I suggest.

"No, not at all. It needs some dancing."

"I don't think these people are the dancing type."

"Nonsense. They're just waiting for someone to lead the way. Shall we?"

"Chance, I don't dance."

"Of course you do."

With that, he grabs my hand and pulls me to the center of the floor and leads me in a ridiculously exaggerated dance to whatever up-tempo inanity is blaring from the stereo. The performance is greeted with cheers and whistles, and then, amazingly—I have to hand it to Chance—others slowly begin to join us. Ten minutes later, the group of displaced refugees is looking an awful lot like a group of teenagers having a good time. Maybe these kids aren't so hopeless after all. All they needed was a leader to show them the way.

Hamilton

A hostess shouldn't spend her party hiding in the kitchen, but since this party isn't really my doing, I don't see anything wrong with sitting at the kitchen table eating pretzels and drinking ginger ale. It makes it easier for Shelly to find me so that she can tell me she thinks there is someone here that isn't supposed to be, or that I should make an announcement to the effect that anyone caught behaving in a fashion that could be considered nerdy will be dismissed from the party immediately.

"It's just so lame out there," Shelly whines. "I don't blame you for hanging out in here."

"I'm just feeling kind of tired, that's all," I say.

"Oh, tell me about it," Shelly says. "It's like snore city out there."

"I'm sorry my party doesn't meet your standards," I

say. "You're welcome to leave if you're not having a good time."

"What? No, that's not what I meant. I was just saying, well, you know, it's just, maybe for the next party—you'll have one around the holidays, right? Maybe for that party, we could plan it together. I have some great ideas. It would really be a lot of fun."

"Maybe you should just throw your own party."

"Oh, I wouldn't want to move in on your turf like that."

I thought that was exactly what she wanted, but I don't say anything. Although it's fun to see Shelly flustered, I'm not in such a confrontational mood. I still haven't figured out for sure who was behind the guest list. I doubt it was Shelly—it was too subtle to be her doing. Anyway, I do have my suspicions. When you know someone long enough, there's very little they can do to truly surprise you. Part of me wants to ignore it and pretend it didn't happen. I want senior year to be perfect, flawless, and it can't be that way if I have to be the hardass keeping everyone else in line. Then again, if everyone else would just behave, I wouldn't have that dilemma.

"It's just something to consider," Shelly says. "Us throwing a party together."

"Okay, Shelly, I'll consider it," I say. Her face registers shock and disbelief.

"Really?" she says. "I mean, that's awesome. You won't regret it."

"We'll see," I say cryptically.

"Right, well, I've got to get out there and take another

head count. I can't seem to get an accurate count. All the unpopular girls look so much alike it's hard to tell them apart."

Shelly deserts me in the kitchen. Sitting at the table, I can hear the party sounds from the surrounding rooms. It doesn't sound as lame as Shelly claims it is. It feels strange, sitting here all alone, listening to everyone else having fun around me and not being part of it. Normally, I'm in the center of all that. I know I should be out there, that there are only a finite number of parties before the end of the school year. Missing one seems like such a waste, but just thinking about the end brings me down, and I'm in no mood to try and have fun. It's stupid, and I know it, but I can't help it.

"Wait a second, aren't I supposed to be the self-absorbed loner?" Alex asks, standing in the kitchen doorway looking at me.

"I was just taking a break," I say.

"That's not like you, either."

I shrug. I can put on a brave face with the girls, but with Alex there's no hiding. I'm naked, all my emotions on display.

"You pissed about the guest list?" he asks.

"No," I say. "And don't talk about that right now."

"Oh, right, infallible Hamilton. Nothing ever goes wrong in her life."

"That's not what I said."

I should have known Alex figured out I didn't make up that guest list. He's intuitive about things, observant.

There's no way I can hide anything from Alex. He knows me better than anyone.

He sits down at the table across from me. I don't look at him. I stare at the bowl of pretzels instead. What would happen if I just dropped out of school, ran away from home, just brought an end to it all right now? I could go out in a blaze of glory, at the height of my popularity, but would they care? Would they forget me by graduation?

"So it's not the best party you've ever thrown, but that's no reason to drown your sorrows in ginger ale and pretzels. Come out and mingle. Your adoring public is waiting."

"I'm kind of tired of my adoring public," I say. I don't know if it's true or not, but it's one of those things that when I say it, I kind of feel like it might be true.

"Where's Hamilton?" he asks.

"Listen to them," I say. "They're having a good time. They don't need me there."

"Are you kidding? The only reason they're having a good time is because of you. You're the one that made this happen. You brought these people together. Without you, none of this would have happened."

"But I didn't," I point out.

"What, you think because you didn't write the guest list that you're not responsible? First of all, they all think you wrote that list, and at least half of these people wouldn't be here if anyone else put up a guest list and threw a party. Second, you've established a whole tradition for fun. Without you, these people would be hopeless. So it's all your doing, whether you like it or not."

Alex is right. It's my traditions that are carrying this party along. The momentum is so built up that it will take a long time for everything I've established to disappear. Certainly the students of Fidelity High can ride this wave straight to the end of the year, whether I'm there with them or not. Nothing in their lives will change. Hell, even Shelly can't kill this thing off.

Perhaps it's time for me to make that quiet exit, just quietly slip into the shadows and out of their lives forever. Off to other grander pursuits, perhaps, or maybe just gone, maybe just not here. It's an appealing idea. But Alex is right—the self-absorbed loner is his role, not mine.

If Hamilton Best is going to make an exit, then she's going to do it in her own unique way. I've never been one for sneaking about or standing in shadows. So it makes no sense to start now. I will be making an exit for sure, there doesn't seem to be any doubt about that. One way or another I have to leave, but I won't be going quietly. They will notice. They won't have a choice.

OLIVIA

Chance spent almost the entire night out on the dance floor, and he never looked more gorgeous. His smile is huge, genuine, and infectious. I get a warm feeling inside just watching him, just seeing him look so happy. Everyone else seems to feel it as well. The glowing soccer star is the center of the dance floor universe. His delight is all the more glorious with no Donna anywhere in sight. If he can be this happy without her anywhere around, there's hope for me.

"He's a great dancer, isn't he?" Zelda says as she finds me leaning against the wall. She doesn't even have to say his name. Who else could she be talking about?

"Yeah," I agree.

"I just never realized what a nice guy he is."

"Yeah," I say again, wondering where she's going with all this.

"He didn't care that I couldn't dance, and he must have known that seeing us out there would give everyone else the confidence to get up and dance. It was great."

"You danced with Chance?" My voice comes out sharp and slightly hysterical-sounding. How had I missed that? It must have happened before I tracked Chance down, or maybe I was so focused on Chance that I hadn't noticed anyone else around him, not even the girl he was dancing with.

"Yeah. Nobody was dancing, and he dragged me out there with him. It was so much fun."

My gut reaction is to be jealous of Zelda. After all, Chance chose to dance with her instead of me. But then I think about what she said, about him being a nice guy, and it all makes sense. He didn't dance with Zelda because he liked her in that way. He was just being nice to her, and he knew that if people saw Zelda out there on the dance floor, they would want to get out there and shake their thing as well. It's proof of his intelligence as well as his kindness.

"He's a really nice guy," I say. "Really nice."

Watching him, and thinking about the way he's so considerate—not just of Zelda, but of everyone—I'm filled with pride. It feels like he's already my boyfriend, not just some guy who likes me despite already being attached to an obnoxious little social climber. It feels so real that I almost forget it isn't, and never will be if I don't take decisive action. After all, the last time Chance saw me, my lips were locked on Alex Journer's.

"Hey, Zelda, can you hold this for me?" I hand her my drink and head out onto the dance floor. I have to dodge flailing arms and spastic legs as I weave my way through the crowd toward Chance. He turns away just as I'm almost up to him, and at the same time someone grabs my arm, stopping me in my tracks.

"So you finally made it out onto the dance floor," Alex says, a little too chummily, in my ear. He's close enough for me to smell the alcohol on his breath.

"Not now, Alex," I say, and turn to walk away, but he clutches my arm.

"Olivia. Listen, about what you said before, I'm—"

"Can we have this discussion at another time?"

"Nobody wants to talk about anything," he says. "What's with you?"

"Well, Alex, it's called a party, and it's a time for having fun, not for having serious discussions."

"Fun, huh? And I suppose you're thinking you're going to have fun with Chance? What happened to you being all on your own, Olivia?"

"In case you didn't notice, Chance is all on his own tonight as well. I was just going over to say hello. You can let go of my arm now."

He does. Then he looks at me with that stupid sad puppy dog look of his. Alex might be tolerable if he could stop being so Alex-like all the time.

"Hamilton was sulking about the party before," Alex says.

"Not now."

I walk away, but it doesn't matter. Chance is gone. I missed my opportunity. He was out on the dance floor forever, but I wasn't quick enough and he slipped away, off to the bathroom or for refreshments or to cool off with a bit of fresh air. It doesn't really matter where he is. All I know is that Zelda got to feel like Cinderella at the ball, and I feel like Cinderella the scullery maid scrubbing the floor.

I step into the kitchen, a good place for a scullery maid, and find it inhabited by Hamilton. I suppose she's kind of like my wicked stepmother. She gives me a lopsided smile, and I wish I'd chosen some other part of the house to feel sorry for myself in.

"Pretzel?" she asks. "As mood elevators, they're kind of lousy, but they're nice and filling."

I take one of the proffered pretzels and lean against the counter, munching. I think of Zelda, who I left holding my drink, and feel a little bit bad, but not that bad. After all, she danced with Chance.

"I think your boyfriend's looking for someone to dance with," I say.

"He prefers to dance alone," she says.

"Could have fooled me," I say. She makes a sort of snorting sound that might be a laugh.

"Is it a fun party?" she asks.

"You could go see for yourself," I say. "You were invited."

"That's interesting, because I didn't see my name on the guest list."

"Your name's never on."

"That's because I usually write it."

"I could play stupid and act like I don't know what the hell you're talking about, but I've known you too long to do that to you. Besides, I don't have the energy."

"You've always been honest," Hamilton says. "Sometimes a little too honest. Not that I'm complaining."

"So?"

Hamilton looks at me, her eyes taking me in from head to toe, like a guy sizing me up, trying to figure out what I look like divested of my clothing, but her undressing is of a different sort. Strip away all the bullshit, and somewhere down there is the truth. She might need a shovel, but she'll find it eventually.

"So, what?" she says.

"Well, you must be pissed," I say.

"Pissed? No. I was at first, but actually, you've been so helpful. It's put things in perspective for me."

"I don't follow."

"It just helped me to see things. That's all." Hamilton takes a pretzel out of the bowl and begins to break it up into smaller and smaller pieces, very methodically. I don't think she even realizes what she's doing. "God, can you believe that this is almost all over? We've been through so much, right from the very start, right?"

"From kindergarten," I say.

"Well, and life begins with kindergarten, doesn't it? I know I can't remember anything before that."

"I suppose you just sprang out of somebody-or-other's head, a fully formed five-year-old."

"Absolutely," she says.

I'm sorry I decided to join Hamilton's mopefest in the kitchen, but don't think I can walk away from her now. She is, by ordinary Hamilton standards, a mess. I don't think I've ever seen her so not in control. It's pleasant, in a way, but it's the sort of thing you want to watch from afar, kind of like how a terrorist wants to see evidence of his large-scale destruction on the television news but doesn't want to see the small picture, the victims, the individuals with their blood and their guts and their families. I would have been content to observe Hamilton's downhill spiral from a more distant vantage point. I may hate her, but she's still my best friend.

"When this whole thing is over, we're going to be adults," Hamilton says. "Is that scary or what?"

"I guess it would be scarier if we didn't get older, if we stayed seventeen forever. I can't imagine anything much worse than that."

"I wish I could stay seventeen forever," Hamilton says.

"The whole world's out there waiting for us," I say.

"It's not my world," Hamilton says. "School is my world."

"So, go to college. Then get a teaching degree. You don't ever have to leave school."

"It's not the same. I can't survive out there. I'll never make it."

"You're being a bit dramatic."

"Once I leave this school, I won't be Hamilton Best anymore. I'll just be some nobody, just another nobody in a sea of nobodies. If I'm not Hamilton Best anymore, then I'm no longer me."

For a moment I almost feel sorry for her, can almost see her getting lost and swallowed up by the big ugly world. Then I remember who it is I'm thinking about. There is no world big enough to swallow Hamilton whole. She'll come out of this whole thing stronger and more powerful than ever, no matter what I do. In fact, I wonder if all I'm doing is feeding the monster that's Hamilton, giving her the strength she needs to take on the big scary real world, and not for the first time, I question my own motivations.

Shelly

Missing first period on Monday is inevitable, as I was up until two a.m. planning every last detail of the Holiday Bash—that's the official name it's going by. The guest list is drawn up; the food, the decorations, and the music are all planned. Every *t* has been crossed and every *i* dotted. Hamilton may pretend she knows something about planning parties, but she doesn't realize that I'm a master party planner.

The problem, of course, is that our party is to be a collaboration, which is ridiculous, really. There's nothing Hamilton can contribute to this party that would make it any better, but I have to at least give the illusion of cooperation; I need to convince Hamilton that she has a say in things, even though everything is already decided. So I have to go to her, pretending I need her mighty party-planning wizardry, and then subtly steer her toward making all the decisions that I've already made.

This is called politics, and fortunately for me, it runs in my blood. After all, my great-grandfather was a state representative, my grandfather a committee man, and my own father serves on the township's environmental commission. The Trusts know how to bend others to their will in the most diplomatic fashion.

As I'm taking my time at my locker, due to the fact that there are still about fifteen minutes left of first period and there's no way I want to spend any of them in gym class, an unwelcome sight comes bounding down the hallway. Can anyone tell me why that goon of goons, Chance the soccer geek, is now a guest list darling? Just look at the hapless fool and it's obvious he doesn't belong in Hamilton's circle of friends. He, of course, feels the need to stop at my locker, as he's assumed wrongly that thanks to his recent adoption into the guest list elite, he and I are somehow friends. Dear God.

"Well, well, well," I say. "If it isn't Mr. Saturday Night Fever himself." This, of course, is meant to highlight his dance floor performance Saturday night and is in no way intended as a compliment, but he smiles like an idiot all the same.

"So when's the next party?" he asks.

"As a matter of fact, I'm working on plans for it right now."

"Awesome."

I shut my locker and start to walk away, but he doesn't

take the hint that I have more pressing business to attend to and begins to follow along like a puppy dog.

"So aren't you supposed to be in class or something?" I ask. Screw subtlety.

"Hah. Aren't you?"

"Due to my station, certain privileges are afforded me." Naturally this isn't true, but it doesn't hurt to keep the plebeian types guessing. Unfortunately, shit-for-brains just laughs like I've said something incredibly hilarious.

"It just so happens that I had an exhausting evening and overslept," I add.

"Oh," he says.

"So, if you don't mind…" With a flip of my hair thrown in for good measure, I step neatly into the one room where I know he can't follow. I just hope to Christ he isn't still pathetically waiting for me outside the bathroom when I step back out, but I have to figure even Chance can't be that dense.

"Hey," says the girl at the sink when I walk in. I don't know her name, but damn it if it isn't one of those unpopular girls from the party the other night. What the hell? I'm surrounded by these dorks. This one is studiously doing her hair in the bathroom mirror, and I want very badly to tell her that no amount of primping is going to make her look good, but I hold my tongue in the name of diplomacy. "I had a great time at the party the other night."

"Well, I've been to better parties, but what are you going to do," I say. I don't add that she shouldn't get her hopes up about making the guest list for the next party.

She hopefully understands that her inclusion was a fluke, a one-time deal.

"Wow, I really love your sweater. Where did you get it?"

For a brief moment, I entertain the notion of taking this clueless little tart under my wing and showing her the ways of the world. Lesson number one, The Right Way To Make Small Talk And Make People Like You: do not make ridiculous comments about someone's sweater in the hopes of making them like you. Anyway, I quickly dismiss this idea when I realize how completely tiresome it would be.

"At the mall," I say. "Last year."

Then, instead of hearing the words *fuck you* in the icy tone of my voice, this dimwit actually puts on a little pouty face and says "Oh" in a whiny voice. Give me a fucking break. It's a sweater, for Christ's sake. Do you really expect me to believe that you're that emotionally involved in a dull old piece of clothing? It isn't even a very nice sweater.

I escape into a stall, where I proceed to shut my eyes tightly, hoping to ward off the headache that's fast approaching while simultaneously willing the dumb bitch out of the bathroom. Finally, five minutes later, she complies with my wishes.

"See you 'round," she says in her little sing-songy voice as she steps out of the girls' room. Perhaps she'll run into Chance and the two of them can engage in some dorky flirting together.

Although I manage to avoid any more run-ins with the

underclass for the remainder of the morning, I do notice an alarming trend. People who I never noticed before are looking at me, flashing smiles at me when I make the mistake of making eye contact, and in general acting like we're some sort of secret friends. I can't be sure, but I have the feeling that these nonentities are all people from Hamilton's party. It is bad enough that I had to spend my Saturday night with these people, but now they assume we're somehow equals. The disaster that was the party lives on in a horrifying way.

"They're coming out of the woodwork," I say when I join the others at the lunch table.

"Who's coming out of the woodwork?" Nordica asks.

"All those freaks who never should have been at the party. I feel so dirty. I just want to go home and take a shower."

"Oh, is that what that smell is," Olivia says. I don't dignify her comment with a verbal response, only roll my eyes to let her know how tiresome I find her.

"I'm not sure I understand," Hamilton says.

"They're talking to me," I explain. "They're smiling at me. It's just so completely wrong."

"You're right, that is weird," Olivia says. "I mean, why would anyone be nice to you?"

"You know, if your biggest problem is that people are being nice to you," Zelda says, "I'd say you're doing okay."

"You do seem to be overreacting," Hamilton agrees.

"I don't even know why I bother to try to talk to you people," I say. "None of you even care that there was an extra person at this party, too. I mean, I guess it doesn't really matter if you're going to invite a bunch of losers anyway, but I don't think we should let people get away with things like that. It sends the wrong message."

"Wait," Nordica says. "There was an extra person at the party?"

"An infiltrator," Olivia says. The bitch.

"What's their name?" Zelda asks.

"I don't know," I say. "See, herein lies the problem in inviting a bunch of nobodies. If I don't know any of their names to begin with, how am I supposed to determine the name of the extra person?"

"Are you sure there was really someone who wasn't supposed to be there?" Nordica asks. "I mean, if you don't know who these people are anyway, isn't it possible you made a mistake?"

"I took a head count," I say, trying my best to impress upon them my absolute conviction. "There was definitely an extra head."

"Shelly, perhaps the reason nobody cares," Hamilton says, "is that the party went great with or without this alleged extra person. So it doesn't really matter."

There you have it. The priestess of popularity at Fidelity High School is an utter idiot. If that's her attitude, then is it really such a surprise that things are in the sorry state they are in? It is imperative that she follow my dictates on this holiday party. I have the power to save her from complete ruin, and it's something I'm willing to do out of the goodness of my heart. Besides, by teaming up, she'll have no choice but to share her reign with me. The school's sovereignty will go from absolute monarchy to partnership. Who will be at the helm of this ship of state? Well, there will be Hamilton and her loyal and trusted sidekick, Shelly Trust. That is, of course, until Miss Trust's rising star completes its ascension.

Nordica

Hamilton started the school decorating committee when she was still a freshman. Not satisfied with the tired decorations the school's custodial staff put up each year to celebrate the holiday season, Hamilton organized an army of creative students to help her make and procure new ornaments, and then to decorate the hallways and common areas so that they sparkled and glittered as brightly as the most extravagant department store. Of course, fast forward three years and Hamilton has managed to extricate herself from the chore of hanging decorations by having me attend in her stead. Not that I mind the decorating all that much.

Still, as I help to hang a string of magenta and white Christmas lights above the trophy case, it occurs to me that since the start of her time here, Hamilton has been making her mark on the school. There's a whole list of traditions and improvements that can all be traced back to Hamilton. After over two years of study, however, I have taken absolutely no initiative whatsoever. I have nothing to show for my time at the school. I am somehow expected to fill Hamilton's shoes, but while she's the sort of person who will always be remembered, even years after she graduates, they will forget me quicker than Shelly Trust forgets the name of an unpopular student.

Of course, it isn't too late. I can still make my mark, but I can't think of a single thing I could do to improve the school, except maybe letting someone else take over as the leader of the flock. What does it say about me that my best idea is to step aside?

When the last icicle has been hung by the main office with care, the decorating committee disbands and I step out into the chill November evening to find that I have been left without a ride home. I wonder if Hamilton ever finds herself abandoned so unceremoniously. I doubt it. Of course, I console myself with the thought that my fellow decorators simply assumed Nordica Freemingle would have her own transportation; after all, she is Nordica Freemingle. It's a mildly cheering thought, but I don't really believe it. That argument could be made for Hamilton, but it doesn't make as much sense for me.

It's not much more than a mile to my house from the school, so I bundle my coat around me, shove my hands into my pockets, and set out into the night. Almost immediately it begins to rain, but it's too cold for rain, so frozen droplets sting my face as the wind gusts whip them at me. I stare down at the road beneath my feet as I fight the wind and the icy pellets pelting my head.

The mile-plus walk (really a mile and a half, who was I kidding?) never seemed so long before. Only a short way into it, I wonder if I will ever get home. What if the frozen rain turns into a blizzard and I'm buried in a snowdrift? How long will it be before someone misses me and sends the search teams out? I imagine a search-and-rescue German shepherd finding my scarf sticking out of the snow, and then all the eager wannabe heroes gathering around to frantically dig, only to find, just beneath the surface, my frozen corpse. With the ice and the cold and my inadequate clothing, freezing to death seems a real possibility. It could happen, couldn't it? I try to pick up my pace, but my body protests against the weather.

I should have called someone for a ride home from school. I should have at least peed while I was at school. I need to go now, and suddenly I remember the story that someone told me once about their aunt, or some relative or other, whose bladder burst on an escalator in some department store in the city all because she didn't like using public bathrooms.

I try to remember if the aunt, or whoever she was, died as a result of the incident. I decide I won't let it come to that. If it becomes so bad that I can't hold it anymore, I'll just go in my pants. Surely that indignity is better than death, and what would it matter, since by then I will be soaked to the bone anyway?

I haven't even made it halfway, although I feel like I've been walking forever, when a car pulls up beside me and a window rolls down. I realize that it won't be the weather that does me in, but a local psychopath.

Then Alex says, "You look like you could use a ride."

"It's okay," I hear myself say. "I'm almost home."

"Nordica? Don't be ridiculous. Get in the car."

So, of course, I do. The warm air blowing out of the car's heater feels like heaven. I defrost my hands over the vent.

"What are you doing out at this hour?" he asks.

"I was hanging Christmas decorations at the school."

"And then you decided to enjoy the evening air and walk home."

"Something like that," I say.

"Look at you. You're soaked," he says, and he brushes his hand across the top of my hair, which has gone from ice-encrusted to drowned rat in the warmth of the car.

"I'll be fine," I say quickly, but Alex doesn't take his hand away. "Really," I insist.

Reluctantly, he returns his hand to the steering wheel. We ride the rest of the way in silence, but when we reach my house, Alex says, "Wait." I turn to look at him.

The dashboard lights give Alex's skin a green tint. He looks a little bit scary, but his eyes aren't menacing even though they bore into me as if they can see right through me. Maybe they can. Alex and I have a lot in common—we're both outsiders who got swept up into Hamilton's three-ring circus, and as such we will always find ourselves sitting on the edges, not quite belonging. I think about what Alex said about being myself, and I realize that I don't even know who I really am.

"Do you ever get scared?" I ask.

"I'm scared of lots of things."

"I mean, scared that you don't even know who you are? If it wasn't for Hamilton and the clique, I don't know who I would be. Shelly keeps talking about all these nobodies that were at the party, and I wonder, is that who I am? Am I really a nobody?"

"Of course you aren't," Alex says. I can't tell in the dim light, but it looks like there's a tear rolling down his cheek. But it can't be. It must be a drop of rain.

"Next year, when everyone leaves me, I feel like I just might disappear into thin air. Just turn into a ghost or something."

"Why would you say that?" he asks. I shake my head and shrug my shoulders, then I reach to open the door, but Alex reaches across and stops me. I stare down stupidly at his hand on top of mine.

Then his lips meet mine. I have a moment to panic about the fact that my lips are chapped from the cold and realize that I had a couple of Lindsey's Doritos when we were hanging up the decorations. Then it's happening, and I'm kissing Alex Journer.

I am kissing Alex Journer! I'm absolutely terrified. I'm kissing Hamilton's boyfriend. I clumsily push him away and quickly open the door. I run across the front lawn as if I'm being chased by a pack of wild dogs. When I reach the front door, I look back and see Alex sitting there in the car, the passenger door wide open since I never bothered to close it. He looks so sad sitting there, like such a little boy. I almost want to run right back to him, to hold him, to comfort him, but I know I can't do this. So I escape to the sanctuary of the house.

zelda

"Okay, who's that?" asks Shelly.

"Wyatt Pearson," I answer. "I can't believe you don't know that. He's the treasurer of the student council."

"Woohoo," Shelly says. "Treasurer of the student council. He's practically a celebrity."

"Shut up."

"Okay, who's that, then?" she asks, pointing at some girl running past, a pink scarf trailing behind her on the breeze.

"I'm not sure," I say, and shrug.

"What? I thought you knew all these dorks."

"I think she's a freshman."

"Well, it doesn't matter. I don't think she was at the party."

In case you were wondering, I have reluctantly agreed to help Shelly identify various people whose names she has never taken the time to learn, but who she now sees as potential threats to her popularity, or something like that. Hamilton's party is nearly a week past, but Shelly still hasn't stopped talking about it. Moreover, she hasn't stopped talking about this mysterious extra person, and she's convinced that if she can match all the guest list names up with faces, then she'll be able to recall which face wasn't on the list.

It's ten minutes to homeroom and we've spent the past twenty minutes sitting behind a study carrel in the library, where we have a half-obstructed view of the main hallway and all the kids coming into school and heading off to their lockers, the cafeteria, or the bathrooms. Of course, I realize the whole exercise is ridiculous, but in Shelly's mind it is some hugely important mission. Shelly is a bona fide lunatic, but she's technically my friend. Besides, she has her strengths.

"So, what do you think of Chance?" I ask.

"Well, for one, I think he doesn't have a snowball's *chance* in hell of making it onto the next guest list." She proceeds to laugh insanely at her own not-very-funny play on words. "Get it, snowball's *chance*."

"Yeah, I get it. Seriously, what do you think of him?"

"You know what your problem is, Zelda? You're too uptight. You need to lighten up."

"I'm not the one who's still worried about an extra person at a party that happened a week ago."

"I don't expect you to understand why this is important, but trust me when I tell you that it is, 'kay?"

"Chance was really a star out on the dance floor, and he's got this infectious smile."

"Infected is more like it," Shelly says. "He's a total loser, and that whole soccer thing, give me a break. This isn't Brazil or some other country where they actually give a shit about soccer. If you're gonna be an athlete, you might as well find a real sport. Plus that fucked-up girlfriend of his—"

"He's got a girlfriend?"

"Hello? How can you know all these dorks' names and not know that Donna Lukowski and Chance Avanale are practically joined at the hip?"

"Isn't that the girl with the drinking problem? I thought she was in rehab or something."

"No, she's out now. Anyway, if you ask me, they deserve each other. Just a couple of loser hangers-on. Hey, I know that girl was there, what's her name?"

I look at the girl with the pixie-cut brown hair in the plaid skirt, and I don't know her name either. Although I do remember seeing her at the party, and the other day she was smiling and being all friendly to me down at the guidance office.

"I think she's new," I say. "I don't know her name."

"A new girl and a dork to boot? How in Christ's name could she have been on the list?"

"She seems nice enough, and what makes you so sure she's a dork?"

"Just look at her."

"You can't judge a book by its cover."

"Of course you can. Just look at you."

Ordinarily I would fire back an appropriate retort, but my mind is elsewhere. The way Alex looked at me when I was dancing with Chance. He looked jealous. There was this look of sadness and longing in his eyes. Then there's Chance, with his smile and his carefree attitude, the complete opposite of Alex, and yet so appealing. Just thinking about the warmth of his embrace out there on the dance floor makes me ache to be held in his arms again, right now.

"I've got to go," I say.

"Homeroom's not for another eight minutes."

"I just remembered something I have to do."

But Chance isn't at his locker or anywhere else in the immediate vicinity. Neither, for that matter, is Donna, and my overactive imagination assumes they must be together. I grab my things from my own locker, resigned for once to be early for homeroom. I slam the locker door shut and find myself staring right at the girl with the pixie haircut and the plaid skirt. I jump back in surprise.

"Sorry," she says. "I didn't mean to scare you. It just seemed like you were upset about something, and I wondered if it was something you wanted to talk about."

I may lack Shelly's social skills, but even I can recognize a social climber who's trying too hard. Then again, if I'm right about her being a new girl, maybe she's just desperate for friends. Maybe she doesn't even realize who I am, or understand the peculiar social dynamics at Fidelity

High. Maybe she assumes that if we were at the same party together, then it just makes sense for us to be friends.

Now, if I was Shelly Trust, I would blow this girl off with a flip of my hair, an overloud sigh, and a dramatically upturned nose, but thankfully, I am not Shelly. Therefore, I might as well be the anti-Shelly. Sure, I'm not exactly a merchant of friendliness, but it won't hurt me to be nice to this girl.

"You ever just have one of those days?" I ask.

"All the time," she says.

"Yeah, I think I'm gonna have that sort of day, and homeroom hasn't even started yet."

"Sometimes I just have to remind myself that tomorrow's a new day."

"Yeah, well, optimism and I have never gotten along too well, but maybe I'll give it a try. Hey, listen to me, I'm sounding optimistic already," I say.

She gives a little smile at this, and I figure now is as good a time as any to make my exit. I head off, muttering something about how my homeroom teacher was a real stickler about tardiness, which thankfully for me is a complete lie.

"Well, I'll see you around," the girl calls after me.

Dear God, I hope not. I realize it's uncharitably Shelly-like of me, but I have no interest in palling around with that tiresome chick. In fact, I'm already hoping that she doesn't make the guest list next time around.

Hamilton

The coffee shop's stereo system fills the air with some female vocalist's crooning, which borders very closely on yodeling. Though the Saturday night crowd is thick, the hum of conversation isn't enough to drown out the semi-singing. It's all starting to give me a headache, and so where I normally would have been patient with Alex when he was in one of his funks, I start to feel testy. He sips slowly at his mocha latte without saying a word.

"What's with you?" I ask.

"What are you talking about?"

"You've barely said a word all night."

He shrugs, and before I can point out that shrugging doesn't count, he says, "I've just had a lot on my mind."

"Well, you can share some of it with me," I suggest. "I

mean, last time I checked, that's how the whole relationship thing works."

"Communication is a two-way street," Alex says.

"And what the hell is that supposed to mean?"

"It isn't as if you're always so open and honest with me."

"Like hell I'm not!"

"Oh, yeah," he says. "What about the guest list?"

"What about it?"

"You had no intention of telling me you didn't write it," he says.

I scan the room looking for anyone who might have overheard, but everyone is safely immersed in their own conversation.

"I didn't think you really cared about those things, and besides, you figured it all out on your own anyway."

"That's not the point."

"What is the point?"

"You could have told me about it," he says. "I know you were upset about it."

"I've got things under control. You don't need to worry."

"No, Hamilton, that's not how this whole communication thing works. You're supposed to open up to me, not keep everything locked away."

I feel on the verge of tears. Alex knows me better than anyone, but he doesn't really know me at all.

"We're not doing this now," I say. "Not here. Not out in public like this."

"Why does it matter?" he asks. "Are you afraid that they'll find out the truth? That they'll learn that you're human after all?" He waves his arm around, indicating the crowded coffee shop where several members of our high school class are busy with their Saturday night socializing.

"I'm not having a fight with you in public," I say.

"Fine," he says. "I was ready to go anyway." He stands up. "Let's go."

"Why don't you go home?" I say. "I think I'm going to walk home. I need to clear my head."

"Don't be stupid. Come on, let's go."

"Go ahead, Alex. I'm a big girl. I can take care of myself."

He looks around the coffee shop, slowly, as if he's searching the place for demons and bogeymen that might pose a threat to my safety.

"Who is he?" he asks. "Are you meeting up with someone?"

"What?" I ask. "Now you're being ridiculous."

"Am I? Like I can't tell. Admit it, Hamilton, you've been done with me for a long time."

"You don't know what you're saying," I say. "Just go."

He doesn't say goodbye, just shoves his chair out of the way and stomps out of the place. My lip quivers. There's a giant lump of sadness in my throat and my heart burns with lovesickness. The last place I want to be is sitting in the middle of the coffee shop. I feel so alone, but I'm not alone for long.

A short-haired girl who looks vaguely familiar, but who I don't know, sits down in the seat Alex just vacated and pulls up to the table. I'm too shocked to speak.

"Hi, Hamilton," she says, as if we're old friends. "How are you doing? I saw Alex walk out. Is something wrong?"

Everything is wrong, but I'm not about to tell her that, whoever she is.

"I'm sorry," I say, in my best snooty-but-in-a-nice-way voice. "It's just I'm not much in the mood for talking right now... ah, you know, I'm not sure that I know your name."

"Jasmine," she says, with a trace less boldness. "From the party, remember?"

Shit. I knew that stupid guest list prank would come back to haunt me. For all intents and purposes, I invited this girl to my last party, and yet I don't know her name.

"Jasmine," I repeat. "Of course, I'm so sorry. Look, you know, it's just been a rough night and I don't know where my head is."

"Hey, no sweat," she says. "I totally understand. At my last school, I dated this guy Mike for, like, forever. You know, at first it was all great and I was *so* happy, but then things started turning sour, and he started acting like this total shithead, and I was, like, spending my lunch crying in the bathroom. It was really horrible. So if you ever need a shoulder to cry on, I'm here for you."

I just want this girl to go away. There's something about her. She reminds me of a little gnat, buzzing about my face, her only purpose to be annoying. Where did she come from? What was Olivia thinking, putting her on the guest list? I just want to close my eyes and disappear.

"Well, I appreciate the offer. But honestly, it's nothing like that. Just a little disagreement."

"Sure, well, but that's how these things always start. So, have you and Alex made plans for after high school? You know, college and all that?"

Who the hell does this girl think she is, anyway? I can't believe she's even asking a question like this.

"Look, I appreciate your concern and all, but I'm fine. Really."

She actually looks disappointed at this news, or perhaps it was the icy tone I used to deliver it. It seems like as good a time as any to beat a hasty retreat.

"Oh, are you going?" she asks as I gather up my things.

"It's getting late," I say. "And like I said, it hasn't been the best night."

"You're not walking, are you?"

"Well, actually, I am. It's not far and the weather's nice."

"Are you crazy? It's freezing out."

"I've got a scarf."

Without further ado, I begin to thread my way through the maze of tables to the door, but Jasmine beats me there and opens it for me. This girl gives new meaning to the word clingy.

"I absolutely cannot let you walk home alone," she says. "Let me give you a lift."

We are more conspicuous standing by the door than

hunched over some table, and there are more than a few java-drinking patrons who turn to look in our direction. I do not want to cause any kind of scene.

"If you insist," I say.

"I'm parked just around the corner," she says.

OLIVIA

As I walk down the dark and deserted hallway, a paralyzing thought stops me dead in my tracks. What if I'm doing exactly what Hamilton wants me to do? What if all my efforts to fight her power, to bring her down to size, are not the rebellious plans I think they are? What if, secretly, this is what she wants me to do, maybe has wanted me to do all along? With Hamilton, there's no telling how far back her devious plans stretch.

This thought doesn't exactly spring forth from nowhere. I was reminiscing about my school years when it struck me that everything I've ever done has been exactly what Hamilton wanted me to do. I don't mean that it was always a case of Hamilton telling me to jump while I queried her as to the required height. Hamilton's a subtle and devious bitch. She can make you do all sorts of things without you ever suspecting that you're not acting with free will but are in fact following the script she's subconsciously given you. Not that she's telepathic or anything like that. It's just that Hamilton knows how to get what she wants from whoever she comes in contact with.

So it isn't that hard to imagine that these feelings of complete loathing, which have been building in me for some time, are not so much my true emotions as projections of the emotions Hamilton wants me to feel. Maybe she really wants to be forcibly removed from power. But then the question remains, why? The workings of Hamilton's mind are a mystery to me, but even I doubt there's any reason why Hamilton would want to be dethroned. What possible purpose could it serve? It would make no sense at all.

Perhaps then, for the first time since that fateful first day of kindergarten all those years ago, I'm acting autonomously. Perhaps for the first time since I was taken under Hamilton's huge and sheltering wing, I'm acting on my own in a wholly original manner. Hamilton could keep me down for only so long. It's time to rise up and reclaim my life. It's time to show Hamilton that she is not the all-powerful being she perceives herself to be.

It's time to post the next guest list. It is nearly six thirty and the school is empty. Even the most diehard students have left in search of dinner. It's only me, the janitorial staff, and a sheet of 8 ½ x 11–inch paper containing what tomorrow morning everyone will assume is Hamilton's latest guest list.

Then a clattering noise, something falling or someone dropping something, echoes down the hallway. I stop, hold my breath. I wait to hear more sounds, perhaps the telltale sound of that same someone picking up the dropped object. When I hear nothing, I decide that it must have only been the masking tape giving way on a don't-do-drugs poster in the health room, or rats getting into the candy display at the school store.

I pull the push pin from my pocket, lean an elbow against the bulletin board, then stop, staring at the bulletin board in uncomprehending confusion. Someone beat me to the punch.

How did they do it? Who did it? I need to get a better look at this list. The nearly nonexistent light in the hallway won't allow me to read the names. I think briefly of hunting down a janitor and inventing some very convincing story of why it is imperative that I borrow a flashlight before I remember the mini-flashlight on my key chain. I pull it from my pocket. It's ridiculously small, smaller even than I remember it, but it will have to do. I squeeze and hold it up against the paper to scan the list.

At first, it has the appearance of being a boilerplate Hamiltonian list. Name after familiar name, standard guest list fodder, but then I notice, sandwiched between the school's elite, the names of those whose popularity is suspect or nonexistent. By the time I reach the end of the list—a list more extreme and daring in its choice of students than any I dared draft—I know that Hamilton did not post this.

I am not alone. Someone else shares my desire to see the mighty Hamilton Best fall. The thought should cheer me, but it doesn't. I'm pissed. How dare they? Who do they think they are?

I feel momentarily protective of Hamilton. No, it doesn't make too much sense. She's my friend, my best friend, it's true, but she's also the object of my loathing, the dragon I need to slay. Instead of cheering on the impostor list, I want to rip it from the board and tear it to shreds. Whoever put it there wanted to steal my thunder. This is my quest, not theirs. What right have they to take this from me? I'm Hamilton's best friend, therefore I'm the one who should bring about her downfall, me and only me.

Anyone could have put that list up, but I know intuitively that it was a member of the clique. Who else would have the audacity? Even a student desperate for popularity and the acceptance of her peers wouldn't make the gutsy, potentially suicidal move of overstepping Hamilton's authority. The other kids in the school fear Hamilton as much as they respect her. Posting a fake guest list is just not something they'd do. But none of the girls in the clique are scared of Hamilton, with the possible exception of Nordica, but then, she's scared of her own shadow. This is an inside job.

I reach up to move the impostor list—that is, the other impostor list—but then I recall the names I read there. Clearly, whoever wrote that list is more bold than me. As a whole, the list is more shocking, more daring, but most of all, more damaging to Hamilton than mine is. Replacing this better list with my own will help no one except Hamilton.

I step away from the board, crumpling my own guest list in my hand before dropping it into the maw of a nearby trash can. That's when I hear it again. This time it isn't a clatter but a softer sound, a sort of rustling. I stare idiotically at the trash can and think once again about rats, but I'm the only rat in the hallway.

"Hamilton?" The voice is male, but even so, I assume I've happened upon the conclusion of the who-posted-the-guest-list mystery. Like a serial killer who can't help pestering the police, the guest list poster has been lying in wait for hours just to taunt Hamilton when she shows up to post the real guest list.

"It's Olivia," I say.

Alex Journer steps out of the shadows. I can't read the expression in his eyes. There's no smile of recognition on his lips.

"You're here kind of late," he says.

"Forgot my physics book," I say. He glances down at my empty arms. "I have to go to my locker to get it."

"But your locker's not down this hallway."

Telling the occasional lie or two can be problematical.

"I realize that," I say. "I was looking for a janitor with a flashlight. It's too dark to read the numbers on the lock." I realize that the lie is another stupid one if Alex saw me reading the guest list by the dim glow of my own miniature flashlight.

"I have a little one on my key chain," he says. "Come on, let's try that."

I let out a nearly silent sigh of relief as I follow Alex down the hallway. He didn't see me reading the guest list, but there is one unanswered question, what is Alex still doing at the school? If there is anyone who can be counted on to not stay late after school, I would think it would be the apathetic Alex Journer.

The beam on Alex's miniature flashlight is even duller than my own, and he has to stand close to me as I turn the dial. His breath is warm on the back of my neck, but it makes me shiver. I grab the text book I don't need out of the locker and close the door.

"Thanks," I say with a smile, and turn to leave.

"I'll walk you to your car," Alex says. "It's late."

"I'm not scared of the dark."

"No? What are you scared of?"

"Not passing my physics test, which is exactly what will happen if I don't get home and study." The lie rolls too easily off my lips.

"What about Hamilton?"

"What about her?"

"Are you scared of Hamilton?"

"No, of course not." But I think of my crumpled guest list now sitting in the trash. What if it had been Hamilton and not Alex in that hallway? What if she'd caught me red-handed with my impostor list? I'm not prepared to face her wrath. Alex is right—I *am* scared of her, and that's a problem, because I want with all my heart to bring her down. That's going to mean dealing with her wrath. I'm not ready.

"I'm in love with you," Alex says.

It's not fair. Why can't someone like Chance say those words to me? Why does it have to be my best friend's boyfriend? But I know. I can feel it in my bones. I'm never going to wind up with Chance. It's all Hamilton's fault. Our lives are too intertwined. I hate her. If I wasn't such a chicken, I'd just tell her off once and for all, just break free and live my own life. I'm scared. I'm scared of Hamilton, and I'm scared of being on my own without her.

Alex leans in toward me. I know I should back away. I know I should run. Instead, I close my eyes. Our lips meet, and I pretend I'm kissing Chance. I wonder if this is the closest I'll come to kissing the boy I hunger for. A braver person would go after Chance, tell him how she feels. A braver person wouldn't settle for kissing her best friend's boyfriend and imagining it was someone else. But I'm a coward.

Shelly

Perhaps the only thing worse than first period gym is being forced to play coed volleyball in first period gym. Despite the fact that I protested to Miss Lang that spending the period walking around the gym would give us far more exercise than standing around waiting for a large white ball to come flying at our heads, I was required to join in the ridiculous game. And it figures that my gym class is full of a bunch of those boys who insist on taking the game all seriously, like serving the ball into the net is a big deal anyway.

The ball comes sailing in my general direction and I do one of those movements that makes it look like I'm trying, even though I have no chance in hell of connecting with the ball unless maybe I dive, but that's not happening. The ball bounces harmlessly on the ground and almost immediately, Miss Lang's whistle sounds nearly full blast in my ear.

"Way to go," some jerk snarls. We've apparently lost the game and are now trading sides.

"It's the third time this year," I overhear Melissa Drackett say to Ryan O'Dowd.

"Popularity is a fickle thing," Ryan says. This, of course, makes my ears prick up, and now that the new game is starting it's harder to hear their conversation.

"He's really crushed, though," Melissa says. "I didn't even think he cared about Hamilton's parties."

"Maybe that's why he hasn't been on the list. Maybe she detected too much apathy on his part."

"Do you think? All I know is, he's really upset. He asked if maybe I wouldn't go, you know, in support of him. I mean, I want to stand by him and all, but this is the Christmas party. It's like the best party of the year, you know?"

Then it's like the world stops, and I hear Melissa's words playing again in my head. *Third time this year. Christmas party.* Just wait one second. Does that mean Hamilton posted a guest list without consulting me? I can't believe this.

"Look out!" someone screams.

The next thing I know, a large white object is inches from my face. Slam. It collides with my nose at a speed so great it knocks me to the ground.

Fifteen minutes later, I'm sitting on that awful pea-green vinyl couch in the nurse's office with a plastic bag of ice on my nose while Zelda tries to recite from memory everyone on the guest list.

"Oh, I think that guy who plays football is on there, too," she says.

"Oh, right, him," I say sarcastically.

"You know who I mean, right?"

"Zelda, there's a few guys in the school who play football. You're going to have to be a bit more specific than that. Give me a break, *he plays football*—you don't know his name, really?"

"If you're going to get all nasty about it, I'm going back to class."

"You never go to class. Come on, who else is on it?"

"Oh, um, Denise Cole and Charlie Liebenz."

"Okay, why do you keep naming people I've never heard of?"

"Don't you know Denise? She's the one who draws all those really cool dragons in art class."

"People who draw dragons do not belong on the guest list. This party is going to suck."

It's during my convalescence (my gym-class injury proves severe enough that I must spend second and third period in the nurse's office) that I reach an important conclusion. Hamilton is an evil, backstabbing bitch. I've always gone out of my way to support her and be a loyal friend, but this is it. Posting that ridiculous guest list, without telling me, without consulting me, was like slapping me in the face. I know where she stands, and quite frankly, I've had enough of it. This is war.

I don't speak to Hamilton or any other member of the clique for the rest of the day. I don't show up for lunch but instead leave campus with Debbie and Caitlin to pick up one of those nasty fast food salads, which are still a thousand times better than anything they serve in the cafeteria. Debbie and Caitlin want to talk about the guest list but I blow them off.

"I've been working like mad to make this the best party ever," I say. "It's going to be a winter wonderland theme. You're going to love it. Oh, and the food is all going to be catered."

"But what about Nadia Benhurst?" Caitlin asks. "That porker will eat everything in sight." This prompts the two of them to break out in a fit of idiotic laughter.

"But seriously, why is she on the list?" Debbie asks. "She seems like such a loser."

"In the spirit of Christmas," I say, talking through my ass, "we will be sharing the bounties of our popularity with those less fortunate."

They both seem to eat this up, and Debbie says, "Sounds like the ghost of Christmas Past has been haunting Fidelity."

As I'm walking up from the parking lot after lunch, Debbie and Caitlin hurrying ahead of me because they're all worried about being late for class, I slip on this patch of ice on the walk. I don't fall down, but wouldn't you know, Alex Journer picks that exact moment to materialize out of thin air. I don't know how he does that, but I swear it's spooky how he just seems to appear out of nowhere sometimes. He grabs my arm to steady me, even though I was never in danger of hitting the ground.

"That's a lawsuit waiting to happen," I say, jerking my arm from his grasp.

"Shelly," he says, in that bullshit listen-to-me-I'm-a-sensitive-guy voice of his, "how are you? I heard about your nose."

"I'm fine," I say.

"I was worried when I didn't see you at lunch."

"There's no rule that says I have to eat lunch with the clique every day." God, he is such a smarmy bastard. *I was worried when I didn't see you at lunch*? Give me a fucking break. Then I remember I'm supposed to be nice to Alex, which is harder than it sounds. Still, someone up there must really like me because they've just tossed some big-time prize in my lap. I mean, I've just suffered an injury, and here's Alex to play my knight in shining armor.

I suddenly find that my ankle does not have the ability to support me, and I drape myself across Alex as we hobble up the walkway. The guy doesn't even flinch. He's definitely ripe for the picking.

"To tell you the truth, Alex, I'm kind of upset about Hamilton posting that guest list without telling me. We were supposed to be planning this party together. That really hurt, you know?"

He turns to look at me then with those dark eyes that aren't so much puppy dog eyes as mangy mutt eyes. I hold the stare longer than is comfortable. He looks away, but I can tell already these subtleties are not lost on him.

"I understand," he says. "She doesn't always confide everything in me, either. She's a complicated person."

"Yeah, maybe," I say, then add, in a quiet voice that's still plenty loud enough for Alex to hear, "or maybe she's just a bitch."

By the time we step in through the school doors, I can already feel it. An alliance has begun to form between us. Hamilton, you are going down.

Nordica

Everywhere I look there are icicles and snowflakes. Everywhere. Shelly hasn't missed a spot. She insisted on doing all the decorating herself. I can't imagine what it cost her.

"Where's the township snowplow when you need it?" Olivia asks, dusting snowflakes from a chair by the front door so she can sit down.

"It looks pretty, though, doesn't it?" I say.

"Pretty over the top, if you ask me," Olivia says.

I know what she means. It does have the look of someone trying too hard. It's reassuring to think that maybe I'm not the only one who worries about keeping it all together, about doing the right thing. Maybe even popularity-obsessed Shelly Trust doesn't entirely get it, doesn't have the whole formula worked out. That seems evident from the mood of the party, which isn't nearly as festive and celebratory as one would hope. It's not that people look like they're having a bad time. They just don't look like they're having a good time.

Standing in the hallway, watching them through the living room door, I can't help but notice that girl. I think her name is Jasmine. She's bubbly and overly friendly in a phony kind of way, like she's Shelly Trust's long-lost nerdy twin. I see her scanning the crowd, looking for a familiar face, and I duck out of the doorway before we make eye contact.

"What's with you?" Olivia asks.

"Nothing," I say. "There's someone here who wasn't on the guest list."

"Don't tell me Shelly's gotten to you as well."

"No, but it's true. I just saw her in there."

Olivia looks at me as if I have three heads.

"You surprise me," she says. "I never would have pegged you for the sort of person who memorizes everyone on the guest list."

That's when I realize my mistake, but it's too late to undo it. I'm not sure what Olivia's look means. I decide I need to come up with some sort of explanation.

"It's just, well, you know how Shelly is," I say. "She wanted to go over it with me. See if I could tell her who all the alleged nobodies were, that sort of thing. That Jasmine chick, I know she wasn't on it."

Does she buy it? Does she even care? Am I being too paranoid?

Olivia peeks through the doorway.

"Do you see her?" I ask. I look over the top of Olivia's head, but I don't see Jasmine. She must have gone into a different room. Instead I see Alex, aloof and alone in the corner, and something inside me starts to ache.

"Alex looks bored," I say.

"Drunk is more like it."

"What?"

"Don't tell me you don't know. Alex always self-medicates before Hamilton's parties. It's the only way he can make it through the night."

It only makes me like him that much more. He's human and flawed and he can't deal with his girlfriend's parties, probably can't deal with her so well either. And if her own boyfriend can't deal with her, then maybe Hamilton isn't exactly so perfect after all.

zelda

I've spent the entire evening feeling as if I was trapped in the world's tackiest snow globe. Christmas isn't exactly my favorite holiday, and perhaps the only thing worse than excessive holiday cheer is excessive holiday cheer set to music. Two hours into the party from hell and I've heard three different versions of "Jingle Bell Rock," each one worse than the one before.

"So, where's your elf costume?" Alex asks.

"I seem to have misplaced it along with my Christmas spirit," I say.

"Yeah, tell me about it. That eggnog was completely virginal."

"Not *spirits*, Alex. Oh, never mind."

Alex plucks an iridescent snowflake from the edge of the mantel and watches as it floats languidly to the ground.

"I detect the hand of Shelly Trust," he says.

"Yes, this is her party," I say, then realize this might be the wrong thing to say. When it's all said and done, this is Hamilton's event. "What I mean is, Hamilton let Shelly do all the decorating and food and stuff. Shelly thinks she can do everything so much better."

"And what do you think, Zeld? Is it so much better?"

"I'm not really much of a party person," I say.

He smiles at me, and I'm not sure, but it almost looks like he winked at me. Was that supposed to be some sort of outcast-to-outcast, I-hate-parties-too wink?

I think about the last party, about Chance, who I saw earlier escaping into the basement with a couple of other guys from our class and about as many cups of the virginal nog. I hoped our eyes might meet across the crowded room and it would be like a scene from a bad movie, where some horrible, sappy violin overture drowns out the campy Christmas carols and we run into each other's arms. Then I realized that this felt a lot more like a nightmare than a dream come true. Then I saw Alex.

He's not anything special, not really, but maybe that's what makes him so appealing. He's so real, so easy to talk to. I'm not meant to be with Chance, but Alex is my destiny. I know it. I feel it.

"Well, and how are we enjoying the Holiday Bash?" Shelly asks as she makes her obligatory rounds.

"I just want to know when the bashing begins. Can I start with the stereo, please?"

"Zelda, would it kill you to act normal for once?"

"Maybe we're the only normal ones here," Alex says.

"Please," Shelly snorts. "Don't make me laugh."

"Why, because your mask might crack, revealing the alien face underneath?" I ask, and I get a smile out of Alex.

"Don't humor her, Mr. Journer. She's just jealous because she isn't the one who planned this whole party."

"It's very wintry," Alex says.

"Thank you," Shelly says, and she actually starts doing this googoo-eye thing with Alex. You'd almost think she was the drunk one. She puts her hand on Alex's arm. "I'm glad I tracked you down, Alex. There's actually something I needed a man's help with." Now, of course, the googoo-eye thing makes sense. She needs a favor, and she thinks Alex will fall right into her trap. I'm more than a little disappointed to see that he does. Shelly leads him away by the arm.

The stereo starts playing "Merry Christmas, Baby," and I desperately need to find someplace to barf.

Hamilton

For a parent teaching a child to ride a bicycle, that first training-wheels-free solo ride must be a bittersweet moment. On the one hand, you'd feel a rush watching the kid's backside as he pedaled hesitantly at first, and then with the increasing distance, more and more confidently. There would be this joy in your heart, and pride, and you would be thinking *I did it! I did it! I taught him to ride a bicycle.* But then there's this other part of you, and as you watch him growing smaller and smaller as he rides away from you, you'd realize that he doesn't need you anymore. That after all those hours, after healing scraped knees with kisses and bandages, you were no longer necessary. Thanks, Mom. Bye, Mom.

Superfluous. That's what I've become. It's been true for some time, I suppose, but only now—standing at a party for which I never so much as lifted a single finger (though to be fair, Shelly kept me apprised of all developments in the planning of her Holiday Bash, even pretending to ask my opinion on things), watching the festive merrymakers, all of them entries on a guest list I did not pen—does it strike me that I groomed the clique's members well. Too well. They no longer need me.

If I disappeared, if I suddenly ceased to exist, who would miss me? I'm not saying they won't mourn my passing; they aren't heartless (well, not completely heartless), but life would go on, pretty much on course. Lunchtime squabbles would remain more or less unchanged, with just one less voice joining the fray. The parties would proceed on course, the guest lists would still be posted. The wobble would give way to steady and confident rolling, and without a backward glance, the now-expert rider would speed off into the distance.

OLIVIA

Two days after Christmas, our holiday break in full swing, we're all invited to gather at Hamilton's for a fun-filled night of hot chocolate and sappy movies, or so the great one promises in her invites to the group. It's perhaps a testament to our failings as popular girls that we are not swamped with other plans during our week-long reprieve from the doldrums of school. Only Shelly makes some noise about having to postpone a ski trip that you know was never planned anyway. When I show up at the appointed time, Hamilton is the only one there.

"Where is everyone?" I ask.

"Oh, they'll be here," she says. "I wanted you to come early so we could talk. We haven't talked in a long time."

"Okay. Well then, talk away."

"Olivia, conversations usually involve more than one party."

"Well, how are you on this fine evening? How about this weather, huh?"

"Do you talk to Alex at all?" Hamilton asks.

The question momentarily seizes me with panic. *Jesus,* I think, *she knows.* I regain my composure almost immediately, but I have a feeling it doesn't matter. Hamilton's astute. She must have seen the panic in my eyes, however brief its duration.

"From time to time I have spoken to him," I say.

"And what do you think his feelings are toward me?"

"His feelings?" I repeat, stalling for time. "We don't really have those touchy-feely conversations."

"I've been spending a lot of time thinking about the future, and I just wondered if you had any insights into Alex's thoughts on the subject."

"By future, you mean, what... like the prom, or next year?"

"You've known me a long time, Olivia, and have you ever known me to go back on my decisions?"

"You've never struck me as being wishy-washy."

"When I pick someone, I stick with them, right?"

"Yeah," I say, not adding that she might have been better not to pick Shelly. Well, one could make the argument that she never did pick Shelly in the first place.

"Well, so, I picked Alex, and I have no intention of letting him go, ever."

She definitely knows. She has to know. It's the only

thing that can explain this conversation. When have Hamilton and I ever sat down and had a long conversation?

"No one said you have to, Ham," I say.

"I'm not stupid," she says.

Sweat is pouring out of my body at an alarming rate. I've never felt so claustrophobic in my life. I feel like I'm going to suffocate. I stare longingly at the door as if I could magically teleport myself outside.

"I know the way this all works," Hamilton continues. "We graduate high school and we make all these promises about staying together forever, then we head off to our respective futures, and in two years we lack the power to even imagine the passionate feelings that ruled our lives in our teenage years. We're destined to become figures in each other's pasts, the high school sweetheart we'll talk about years later in patronizing terms."

Her speech has gone in a different direction than I'd anticipated, and though I'm not convinced I'm entirely off the hook, my panic has eased up.

"You're being too hard on yourself," I say. "Plenty of people marry their high school sweethearts."

Plenty of people have high school sweethearts, but Hamilton's the only one of us who has a bona fide boyfriend. It's as if for the rest of us, Hamilton and the clique are supposed to take the place of having a guy of our own, which is complete crap. But I saw it with Chance, the way for a second or two there he was actually interested in me, and then bam, like that, he slipped away from me. I could blame Donna, but it wasn't her fault. It was Hamilton's.

How pathetic is it that the closest thing I've had to a boyfriend is Alex?

"Alex hasn't even brought up that idea," she says. I notice she's slipped off her shoe and is stubbornly rubbing her toes into the floor, as if begging the carpeting to open up and swallow her whole.

"Well, I'm not saying you guys are going to get married this instant. I'm not saying for sure that you will get married, but if he really is the right guy for you, then I don't see why you guys wouldn't get married. Some day. Down the road."

"I can't handle losing him. Do you understand this?" she says.

"Please," I say, "you're the strongest person I know. You could handle catastrophes of any magnitude. A little breakup would be no sweat."

"Without Alex, I think I would just slip away."

I'm about to ask her about this, but she suddenly stops grinding her foot into the floor and looks up. Then I hear them, too, voices outside. I hear Shelly Trust say very loudly, "Pastels are always in style!" Then the doorbell rings.

Shelly

The second-best school day is the day after Christmas break. The first, of course, is the first day of the school year. The two have a lot in common. Both are days of new stuff, new clothes, new toys, and sometimes even new loves. Plus, they both signal the start of something. In September, it's the start of the school year. In January, it's the beginning of the end of the school year.

This year more than ever I'm excited about getting to that last day of school. Well, yes, it's graduation, and that's something to get excited about, but also I see it as my chance to explore bigger and better things. Fidelity has grown stale. I want to move on. High school is small change. I have bigger empires to conquer. First things first, though; I've got one despot to topple.

I've begun to count the days until school ends, crossing them off with a fat red marker in my new Impressionists calendar, because I want to remind myself of how little time I have to bring Hamilton down. I parade into school on January 2 with new clothes, new shoes, and a renewed determination. Nothing is going to stand in my way.

Especially not some pathetic underling in, I kid you not, a cheetah-print dress and plaid tights standing by my locker. No, check that, *waiting for me* at my locker. What in God's name? I can't be sure, but I have a suspicion she's been at the party, one of the parties, maybe all of them. There's something hauntingly familiar about her.

"Hey," she says, far too enthusiastically. "How was your break? What were you up to? Do you ski?"

"What?" I stammer, and I mean to say something curt, but instead, still in a state of shock, I say, "Ski? Who?"

"My break was pretty lame, but I did go down to visit my sister for a few days. She has her own apartment."

"Well, that certainly sounds exciting. I'm so jealous."

"Why? Did you not have fun over break?"

Sarcasm is completely lost on this loser.

"For your information," I say, "I had an excessive amount of fun over break." I'm about to add something to the effect of this not being any of her business in the first place, but the snot cuts me off.

"That's good to hear. It went so fast, but also I guess I'm glad to be back. It's—"

The homeroom bell rings, sending little miss fashion disaster scurrying down the hallway with a wave and some inane chatter about tardiness or some such. I just stand there shell-shocked, staring at the space beside my locker that her body occupied just moments before, trying to make sense of the whole exchange.

"You look like you just saw a ghost or something," Alex says as he saunters past.

"You're going to be late for homeroom," I say, then remember I'm supposed to be trying to get Alex to fall helplessly in love with me. I try to sway him with a swooning look of adoration. It's too forced and it's just as well he isn't paying attention, lost in his cloudy land of dreams once again.

"Wait, Alex," I say. "Did you see that girl in those plaid tights go bolting down the hall a few seconds ago?"

"She was kind of hard to miss."

"Who the hell is she?"

"Not a clue."

"She's been at the parties, hasn't she?"

"How am I supposed to know? Isn't that your job? Aren't you like the princess of popularity or whatever?"

Jesus, this is not working. I want Alex to be flirting with me and making goofy jokes, but he's practically snarling like a cornered animal. What a crappy day. Only he did call me the princess of popularity, even if his tone wasn't what one could call complimentary. And just what does *princess* mean, anyway? Surely he can't be ranking me below Hamilton—am I the princess to her queen? That's hardly the title I'm shooting for. I want to be at her level or just a hair removed, not simply next in line for the throne.

"Did you have a nice Christmas?" I ask, but Alex has already started to walk away.

"Nice?" he says in that sulky voice of his. "Well, I suppose that compared to getting knifed to death by a homicidal maniac, it was pretty damn peachy."

Right, okay. Sorry I asked. Five months. I just have to hang in there five more months and this will all be over.

Nordica

On a cold January evening there's no place I'd rather be than safe and warm in the overheated swimming pool room, the air thick with humidity and the nearly intoxicating aroma of too much chlorine. So this is why, long after everyone else has gone off, changed, and made the mad dash across school to buses or rides, I'm still here in my damp suit sitting on one of the diving platforms and looking down into the cerulean depths of the pool, its glassy surface calm now after the storm of practice this afternoon. I play idly with the swim cap in my hands and stretch my foot down until my toe breaks the perfect surface and sends a series of ripples radiating across the water.

It hasn't been a good week. Everyone is so cranky and moody. Maybe it's seasonal affective disorder. Maybe it's hormones. Or possibly everyone feels the way I do, that vacation was too short, that they want to be anywhere else but here, trudging on through the long, dark winter until the impossibly far-away spring arrives to fill us with the hope of summer and the promise of good things waiting just around the corner.

Of course, it's more than just the thought of winter dragging on forever that has me feeling down. It's two other things that are really the source of my abysmal mood. The first is Alex Journer. It isn't Alex himself who brings me down, anything but. It's the fact that I know I will never have Alex Journer—that this can never be, not in a million years. This is a problem, since I've decided I'm madly, totally, and completely in love with Alex. The second thing that's got me feeling like a squirrel whose spinal chord has been reduced to jelly thanks to a full-body massage by an eighteen-wheeler is Hamilton, who I've decided I hate from the bottom of my soul.

I used to like to sit at the bottom of the pool, practicing holding my breath and enjoying the silence that exists beneath the water. I'd imagine the underwater kingdom that was my real home, my true home, not this drab world of split-level houses and smoke-spewing automobiles. I'm homesick for that fantasy world now. Staring down into the pool, I can almost see it. If I squint hard enough, the lane markers seem to dissolve and a strange city of sand and shells takes on a hazy sort of shape, like a mirage in the desert. I scoot over to the edge of the platform, ready to fall down into the pool, ready to dive down to the bottom to sit and enjoy the stillness, to seek out the mysterious, enchanted world that calls to me.

I jump when the door opens. I'm so close to the edge that I almost fall in by accident, but I'm able to stop myself and slide back safely onto the platform, now looking into the darkness at the far end of the room to see who has joined me. Footsteps echo on the tile floor, and I think it might be Coach Lerner coming back to pick up something she's forgotten, or maybe to shut off the rest of the lights.

"I know you wrote that list," my companion says, and Olivia steps out of the shadows on the other side of the pool.

The warm and humid air feels suddenly cloying. I can't speak. I can barely remember how to breathe. I remember how I slipped up at the party.

"It took me a little while to figure it out, but then it all made sense," she says. "Well, most of it made sense."

"Olivia, hey," I say, stalling for time. I look back down at the pool. It's not too late. I could jump in. I could sink to the bottom, where I'd be alone, blanketed by silence. It's tempting, but it won't work. I'd have to come up for air at some point, and there Olivia would be, waiting for me.

"I'm not sure what you're talking about," I say.

"Hamilton didn't send me here, if that's what you're thinking," she says. "She doesn't know about the list. Well, I mean, obviously she knows she didn't write it, but she doesn't know who wrote it. I mean, maybe she figured it out, but I don't think so."

"I don't expect you to understand," I say. I speak softly,

but the acoustics of the room are such that Olivia can hear me loud and clear.

"Oh, but I do, see, that's the thing. You beat me to the punch."

"I'm not sure what you're talking about."

"I wrote my own list. I snuck into the school at night to post it, but yours was already up, and I had to throw my list out. Yours was much better."

"I don't believe you," I say.

"We're on the same side," Olivia says. She leans against the stainless steel railing of the pool ladder. "I'm as sick of this shit as you are."

It didn't make any sense. What reason did Olivia have to make up a fake guest list? She has everything going for her, and she's been Hamilton's friend, her best friend, for longer than any of us. And then maybe I do understand, just a little. I've known Hamilton just two and a half years, and I hate her tremendously. Olivia has known her nearly her whole life. What sort of emotions could build up in a person in that time? What sort of hatred could develop when the object of that hatred was none other than Hamilton Best herself? I hate Hamilton Best, but Olivia must feel positively murderous.

"I don't know what you're talking about," I say, but even I'm not very convinced by my words.

"It can be our own little thing," Olivia says. "Top secret."

"Like we're spies?" I ask. The room feels like it's grown suddenly cooler. Maybe the heaters are on some sort of timer. I can't wait to get out of my swimsuit and into warm, dry clothes.

"Double agents," Olivia says. "You're perfect. You have such an innocent face."

I'm tired of being the girl with the innocent face.

"So, what now?" I ask.

"She's vulnerable right now," Olivia says. "We have to strike while the iron is hot."

"Hamilton has never in her life been vulnerable. People like Hamilton can't even comprehend vulnerability."

Olivia sighs. "I see she has you as mesmerized as the rest of them. Hamilton is only as strong as people think she is, and as long as people don't see her as strong, present company included, then she's nothing but a frail and helpless enemy ripe for the conquering."

I think about this, about how it would feel to be free of Hamilton. To be free of the pressure to be this thing that I'm not, this popular girl, expected to lead and inspire. I imagine what it would feel like to be released from this prison, and it's almost as alluring as that mysterious mermaid village beneath the water. I don't have to do this all on my own—with Olivia's help, together we could make our escape and it would be swift and smooth.

"What makes her so vulnerable right now?" I ask.

"She's preoccupied," Olivia says. "She's worried about graduation. She and Alex had that fight, and she's very dependent on him, too dependent. She's scared shitless."

"Hamilton and Alex had a fight?" I ask, and in my surprise my cool calmness disappears, emotion creeping into my words.

"A big one, apparently. Over break. New Year's Eve. Didn't you notice Alex moping around? Stupid question. He's always moping around."

"I guess I thought he was just in a crappy mood like everyone else."

"I'll tell you a secret. Alex is a smart guy, and I think he's realized he might be better off without someone like Hamilton Best. Whatever the case, I know for a fact that he doesn't need her half as much as she needs him."

Then, for the first time all week, that big lump of unhappiness that took up residence in my chest suddenly shrinks a bit. The euphoria tastes sweet on my tongue. Alex. Maybe things aren't as bleak as I thought. Maybe, just maybe, I have a chance, and any chance, no matter how small, is worth it. If Olivia had told me right then that she wanted me to shoot Hamilton Best dead, I would have done it, I swear to God I would have. But luckily for me, luckily for Hamilton, her plans are not quite so dramatic.

zelda

Somebody started a countdown in fuchsia lipstick on the mirror in the girls' bathroom upstairs near the library, the bathroom that I utilize to avoid math class. Today it reads *118 DAYS UNTIL PROM*. What's scarier than the fact that someone is so devoted to this countdown that the days have been kept accurate—that someone continues to rewrite the message daily, after, no doubt, a dutiful custodian wipes it clean every night—is that for the first time in my life I actually care.

Of course, my first reaction to the message was to scoff, but then I started thinking about it. At first, 118 days seems like a lot, like a really long time, but keep in mind that it counts weekends too, and that there really is so much to do to prepare for the prom. I mean, the biggies are securing a date and finding the perfect dress, but there are the smaller details too, not just the hair and the nails, but determining who will be sitting at your table, whether you will be driving to prom or splurging on a limo, whose house you'll be meeting up at, how much time to allow for picture taking. Really, there are a lot of details, and as that countdown reminds me daily, my time is growing shorter.

I know, I know, I'm Zelda Winston. I'm not supposed to care about these sorts of things, and a part of me doesn't, a part of me knows how ridiculous it all is. But this other part of me is trying to figure out how the hell I'm going to get Alex Journer to ditch his present prom date and ask me to go in her stead. It's too bad Alex doesn't spend more time hanging out in girls' bathrooms or he might also find the bright pink message a tad alarming, and maybe, just maybe, it would jar him to his senses.

"I've searched every restroom in the school looking for you." Shelly Trust bursts into the bathroom with her usual whirl of exuberant energy, and it's clear that she feels I'm somehow to blame for not having been in any of the other bathrooms she checked. She catches sight of the lipstick note and pulls out an eyeliner pencil to add this postscript: *It's too late, you've got no date, loserdom is your fate.*

"Clever," I say. "Are you the one that's been keeping the countdown?"

"Please," she snorts. "I've got better things to do with my time."

"Like make up stupid rhymes."

"Don't start with me, Zelda."

"By the way, who are you going with to the prom?"

"I haven't made a decision yet, but I promise, if you're nice to me, I'll pass my runner-up on to you."

"You're assuming I don't already have a date."

"Second cousins from Sheboygan don't count."

"He goes to Fidelity," I say. "He's quite desirable."

"He can't be that desirable if he's taking you to the prom."

"He's discerning."

"Cough it up."

"I don't think so. I'd prefer you didn't meddle."

"Fine. Whatever. I don't have time for this."

Shelly proceeds to primp and preen in the scribbled-on mirror, ignoring me but not having much luck ignoring the message that keeps getting in the way of her hair styling.

"Oh, by the way," she says, "I need you to do me a little favor."

"I hope you're joking."

"You know that girl, the one who dresses like a freak?"

"You're going to have to be more specific," I say. "That includes ninety percent of your friends."

"Ha ha. The one Hamilton insists on inviting to all the parties, all chatty and perky, a little too friendly."

"Okay, yeah, I know her."

"I need you to become friends with her," Shelly tells me.

"What the hell are you talking about?"

"Obviously the little loser is desperate for a friend, and

who better to handle the task? No offense or anything, but it would just look weird if I was trying to be her friend."

I feel like saying it would look weird if Shelly was trying to be anyone's friend, but I keep my mouth shut. I'm concerned she might fly off the handle.

"From where does this sudden sense of altruism spring?" I ask.

"We need to get into her confidence," she says. "That girl has the potential to be a very useful person."

"Maybe I'm not comfortable with using people."

She seems to contemplate this, or else she's contemplating her hair, which seems to be a few strands away from being absolutely perfect.

"Whoever he is," Shelly says, in a voice that's gone quiet and conspiratorial, "this desirable guy, I'll make sure you're on his arm come prom night. I just need you to do this one little favor for me."

"Okay," I say, even though I don't know how I could ever tell Shelly or anyone else that the guy of my dreams is the guy of Hamilton's reality, but I'm so desperate, so hungry for him, that I'm ready to run off like an obedient dog to retrieve her mistress's slippers. "I'll leave you and your hair in private. I've got a social misfit to befriend."

Then I walk across the bathroom, stopping at the door to look back at Shelly. She looks away from the mirror long enough for her eyes to meet mine, sealing our agreement. How messed up am I that I'm willing to make a deal with this she-devil just because there's an outside chance it will deliver Alex Journer as my prom date?

I decide not to waste time worrying about how, exactly, I'll break the news to her who my mystery man is. It's more fun to focus on the positive . . . like how perfect it will be to glide across that dance floor with Alex.

Hamilton

Valentine's Day is nearly a month away, but I've learned my lesson. If I wait too long to post a guest list, someone else will be kind enough to do it for me. While there's a good chance that they'll post a list as horrendous as my own, there's also the possibility that they won't go low enough to scrape the barrel's very bottom. The guest list that I pull out of the computer lab printer is atrocious. Oh, I've been sure to include Fidelity's most elite students—they have to be there to witness the travesty, because popular girls are kind of like trees in that regard. Our demise is not real unless we have an audience. Beheadings are always public spectacles.

I walk out of the computer lab and straight into Alex. I don't know how long he's been standing there. Perhaps he's been watching me the entire time.

"Working on a paper?" he asks.

I hold the guest list down, out of view.

"I didn't think you generally stayed after school," I say.

"I don't, but you weren't at home, so I came back. I need to talk to you."

"What could you possibly have to say to me, Alex?"

I push past him and walk briskly down the hall, head held high. I don't look back. I refuse to let the tears that are forming in my eyes fall down my face. Alex trots up to me, then plants himself in front of me.

"Don't do that," he says. "Don't walk away from me. Don't ignore me."

"Don't tell me what to do," I say.

"Why? Because you're Hamilton and nobody dares to cross Hamilton?"

"No, because you're nothing to me, Alex. You said as much to me New Year's Eve, or don't you remember?"

I've tried not to think about our fight. I've tried not to think of what Alex said that night, and I haven't thought about it, not consciously at least. But it's been there this whole time in the back of my head, gnawing away at me. How can I not think about Alex when he's been my anchor for so long?

I try to push past him again, but he holds me back with one hand. I could push him away, but I don't. I don't want to. I want Alex to hug me, to fold his arms around me, to cling to me tightly and never let me go. He doesn't. We only stand there, an arm's length apart. He holds me, but also holds me away.

"That's not what I said and you know it," he says. He sounds like I feel—like he's going to cry. Part of me wants him to let go and cry, to give me the strength to let my own tears fall, but the other part of me, the part that's made of steel, knows it's best for both of us if we don't give in to our emotions. "What am I supposed to do when you force an ultimatum on me like that?"

"Ultimatum? Since when is asking someone to love you and stand by you an ultimatum?"

"Forever, Hamilton. You asked for forever."

We had been alone, at Alex's house. Beside us the Christmas tree glowed with multicolor lights. The television was on and Times Square revelers were busy whooping it up. I was holding the hand of the boy I loved, of the boy who loved me, and it all felt so fleeting. I could feel him slipping away. I could feel it all coming to an end. I knew I couldn't handle it. I couldn't handle losing Alex.

"Alex," I'd said, "I need you to love me and stand by me. I need you to promise to always love me. I need you to promise to never leave me."

Then Alex said the words that tore through my soul, the words that sealed my fate, our fate. In that room that seemed almost overcrowded with holiday cheer, so much so that it had become desperate and gloomy, sitting on that couch waiting for the new year to begin, Alex spoke those four words that felt like someone shoving a knife into my heart.

Alex said, "I can't promise that."

So, how can I reconcile that with what this other Alex

is saying, here in the hallway outside the computer lab: "I love you, Hamilton. I love all of you." It just doesn't add up.

"Do you understand me?" he asks.

"No, Alex, I don't think I do."

"No," he agrees. "How could you? How could you ever understand. That's the whole problem."

"Alex, I've got to go now. It's over."

OLIVIA

The universe has certain rules that should never be broken. Though it's nowhere near the top of the list of inviolable rules, it's still a biggie: broken-hearted girls should not throw Valentine's Day parties. This is perhaps the worst party I've ever been to in my entire life. There are reasons certain people are not invited to traditional high school social events, and if you think I'm bitter that Hamilton beat me to the punch with her latest guest list, well, you're right, but it's still a shitty party, no doubt about it.

Then again, I suppose that's the point. Hamilton has more brains than I give her credit for, and when she saw what I was trying to do, she dove in with both feet. It's been that way my whole life, so I don't know why I expected it to change now. She's always been two steps ahead of me, charging on ahead while I'm still busy looking over my shoulder.

As if she could hear my thoughts (who knows, maybe she can), she shows up beside me and throws a chummy arm around my shoulder. She smiles one of those big Hamilton smiles at me, though this one is a little too big, a little too bright, and for the first time in, well, maybe, ever, I can see behind the mask. I can see the hurt little girl she is trying so hard to hide.

"What do you think?" she asks.

"Worst damn party I've ever been to," I say.

"I know. Isn't it awesome?"

"I don't get it, Hamilton."

"What's not to get?" she asks. "This is what you wanted after all, isn't it? Look." She points across the room. "Even Chance is here to see it all."

"Stop pointing," I say.

"What, you like him, don't you?"

Chance sees us looking at him. It's kind of hard not to notice, with Hamilton pointing like that. He puts on a brave smile and offers a friendly wave, but even from across the room I can see how miserable he is. Hamilton's awareness of my secret crush surprises me, but I know it's just one more case of me never getting one over on Hamilton. She is, and forever will be, the mighty Hamilton, and I am just Olivia her faithful lackey.

"I didn't know you knew," was all I can manage to say.

"Please," she says, and shakes her head. "You're like an open book, Liv, and Alex is always going on and on about Chance and getting all steamed up, so of course I figure you must have a thing for him. For Chance, I mean, because I know how Alex feels about you."

"You should have invited him," I say, referring to Alex, who for the first time has not made the guest list.

"I'm sure he'll show up anyway."

She's right, of course. Thanks to the note I left in his locker, Alex will be here right about... I look at my watch. Well, if he was punctual, he should already be here, outside on the back patio sharing a hot chocolate and maybe something more with Nordica. I intend only to take a picture, to leave it anonymously in Hamilton's locker—unlike my note to Alex, which I signed with my name even though I had no intention of being at the rendezvous spot. Alex might be surprised to find Nordica there instead, but I don't think he'd be entirely disappointed.

Now that Hamilton is here, though, so determined to have the last laugh, why waste a golden opportunity?

"It's kind of stuffy in here. I'm going to step out for some air," I say. "Why don't you join me?"

"That sounds refreshing," she says.

She follows me out the back door. I was hoping for something more dramatic, but it's incriminating enough, I suppose. The two of them are sitting on the top patio step, the inky blackness of the backyard stretching out beyond them like some deep, dark ocean. Alex has his arm around Nordica. Nordica rests her head on Alex's shoulder. They're both bundled up in coats, hats, and gloves, even though it doesn't feel all that cold outside. They jump when they hear us and quickly move away from one another, which is more incriminating than the two of them sitting there.

"So," Hamilton says. She looks at Alex. She looks at Nordica. Finally, she looks at me. "This the best you could do?" she asks me.

"I don't know what you're talking about," I say.

"It's not like what you're thinking," Alex says, a sure sign that it usually is exactly like what one is thinking, or possibly worse.

"I don't remember seeing your name on the guest list, Alex," Hamilton says. Her voice is flat, cold, emotionless. I feel disappointed. If not tears, I'd hoped for rage, at least. But not from Hamilton, not from the girl who has it all under control.

"I thought you said her name was Jasmine. She's not on the guest list."

We all turn around to see Shelly dragging an unwilling Zelda outside. The two of them look up, as surprised to see us as we are to see them.

"I guess this is where the real party is," Zelda says, wrenching herself free from Shelly's grasp. "Hi, Alex."

"Zelda," he says with a nod.

"Does nobody pay attention to guest lists anymore?" Shelly asks.

"I haven't set foot inside," Alex says.

"I wasn't picking on you," Shelly says. "I mean, I know you and Hamilton have your differences, but I don't think she should have excluded you from the party."

"I think he's been having more fun out here, anyway," I say. "If you'd come out here just a few seconds earlier, you would have caught him making out with Nordica."

Alex shoots me a look that makes me wish I were bundled up in winter gear.

"That's not true," Nordica says. "We were just talking."

Zelda takes the whole thing in like a spectator at a tennis match. Hamilton stands there cool and calm. Her arms are crossed over her chest and she just watches and waits to see what I'll say next, but I have nothing left to say.

"Don't worry, Nordica," Shelly says. "No one will actually believe that Alex and you have a thing. I mean, you're not his type. He likes upwardly mobile popular girls, don't you, Alex?"

"I wouldn't expect you to understand," Alex says. "But clearly I've worn out my welcome. Good night, ladies."

He jumps the last two steps to the ground and disappears into the darkness.

"So," Hamilton says. "What's this you were saying, Shelly, about someone not being on the guest list?"

Unbelievable. She's just going to try and pretend that nothing at all had happened. I feel so cheated.

"I think she was on there," Zelda says. "I mean, she was on all the other guest lists."

"No she wasn't," Shelly says. "I've studied them. She wasn't on a single one."

"You studied the guest lists?" Nordica asks.

"Who are we talking about?" Hamilton asks.

"Jasmine," Zelda says. "And she's definitely been at all the other parties this year."

"That explains it!" Shelly shrieks. "She's been the extra person. She's the uninvited guest!"

I stare at them all as if I'm watching actors on a stage. I feel so removed from all of them. I can't even begin to bring myself to care about this stupid little debate. I can't even remember why I ever cared about something as stupid as a guest list. It's all such nonsense, and as I think about the past few years, it's all been like this. All the stuff that I thought mattered, all the stuff that kept me awake at night, is nothing but a bunch of balderdash.

No wonder Hamilton didn't care when I tried to upset the whole house of cards on her. She knows better than any of us what a load of bullshit it all is. She has us all beat by a mile there. The guest lists, the parties, Chance—it doesn't mean a goddamn thing. Alex is perhaps the one exception, for her, but even that didn't work. I'm too late. She has already washed her hands of Alex. She doesn't need him anymore, and, I realize, she doesn't need me anymore either. None of them do. If I were to just slip away, they wouldn't notice. If I just quietly disappeared into the darkness, who would care? They would keep up this debate about some girl who wasn't on the guest list for who knows how long.

I take a step backward, and another, and another. I feel a twinge of regret. I think of Chance's brave smile, his friendly wave, but Chance is just something I can never have. I take a final step, and then I am gone.

Shelly

The whole problem with Hamilton and her guest lists is that everybody knew about the party even if they weren't one of the exclusive few who made the list. And as we saw with the top candidate for worst-dressed person at Fidelity High School (and that's including the ancient home ec teacher and her even more ancient polyester blouses), that left the door wide open for interlopers to come crashing on in. However, when one has a by-invitation-only soirée and hands out invitations to those she's chosen to attend, feckless losers are in the dark about the party. What they don't know about, they can't crash.

The other thing I realized, and I feel like a major moron for taking so long to do so, is that the sure way to beat Hamilton at her own game is simply to throw a better party than the queen of popularity herself—not hard to do judging by her past few efforts. There's no law that says Hamilton is the only one permitted to throw parties.

The invitations (cream cardstock with gold edging, in gold foil–lined envelopes) to my Pot of Gold Fête were handed out two days ago, and already, judging by the warm reception and the flood of RSVPs, everyone is excited about the prospect of a party that will truly be one of the most memorable ones Fidelity has ever seen.

Even Hamilton seems to have realized my rightful rank as the real popularity queen of the school. I'm proud of her for taking what must surely be quite a blow so gracefully. She's already RSVP'd and says she's looking forward to it. Naturally, I've invited only the most popular students, and I think Hamilton will see the error of her ways when she sees how wonderful this party will turn out, and who knows, maybe if it all goes well, she could help me out with the next party.

Walking down the path to the student parking lot, mentally preparing a shopping list of all the items I'll need to purchase for the party, I catch a glimpse of a familiar figure shuffling along ahead of me.

"Alex?"

He stops and turns around, giving me one of those half smiles. It's strange, but I'm starting to see more of what Hamilton saw in him. Don't get me wrong, I don't have a crush on him or anything like that. I mean, he's too skinny, and the sad puppy dog thing can get a bit old a bit quick, but still, there's something about him—I mean, if you go for those dark, brooding types.

"Shelly?"

"Did you get my invitation?"

"It's in my backpack."

"You haven't RSVPed yet."

"I think I might sit this one out. I'm kind of partied out."

"Hamilton will be there."

"I'm sure she will."

"Look, you guys have to get back together. It's just not natural, the two of you being apart."

"Well, you can put in a good word for me, then."

He starts to walk away, but I put my hand on his arm to stop him. He stops and looks down at my hand.

"Please come to my party," I say.

"Shelly?" he says, and looks at me expectantly.

I let go of his arm. He stares at me with those sad eyes, like maybe he might just pour out his whole soul to me right here and now. I don't want to look down at my watch, but I want to go to the party supply place and I'm thinking Alex might have one of those souls that it could take a long time to pour out.

"Look," Alex says. "If you talk to her, at all—I mean, I don't know if you guys talk, but if you do, just tell her I'm sorry, and I love her, but I'm just one person."

I don't know what the hell that's supposed to mean, but I nod and agree to pass on his message, relieved that I didn't get stuck being his shoulder to cry on for the duration of the afternoon.

"Hey, what were you and Alex talking about?" Zelda

asks, bounding down the path toward me. It's weird, but Zelda, whose wardrobe as far as I knew consisted of nothing but shades of gray and black, is wearing a pink sweater. It's not an especially stylish sweater, but still, it's pink, which seems like a pretty big step in the direction of normalcy. Perhaps she's finally beginning to learn, under my direction. It just goes to show you the value of a good teacher.

"Just talking about my party."

"Jasmine heard about it, by the way," Zelda says. "I don't know from who. She's wondering when she'll get her invitation."

"I trust you told her when hell freezes over."

"I didn't have the heart. Besides, I wasn't sure what you were planning."

"Well, I was planning to humiliate her in front of the entire school, but there's really no point now. Just let her know that I have no interest in being her friend, and provided she stays away from me, she won't get hurt."

"We did have a deal, remember."

It takes me a moment to remember what I promised to Zelda. That's right: if she was friendly with Jasmine, I was going to secure her prom date. Well, it's not an entirely impossible task, and with my popularity star in the ascension it shouldn't be too much trouble, but this is Zelda Winston we're talking about. Of course, the pink sweater gives me hope.

"Who is he?" I ask.

She doesn't answer, but looks longingly down the path.

Alex has long since rounded the corner and disappeared from view, but as there's no one else out there, I can pretty much guess what her wistful stare means.

"You've got to be kidding me," I say.

"What?" she asks.

"Okay, okay," I say. "You're crazy, you know that?"

She shrugs.

Nordica

I've been avoiding everyone ever since Hamilton's Valentine's Day party. Partly it's because of what happened with Alex, even though nothing really happened with Alex. I mean, I know Olivia had this grand plan, how we were going to bring Hamilton to her knees or whatever, but the thing is, I could never do that to Alex, use him like that. He's a nice guy, and even though I kind of like him, I didn't want it to be like I was pretending to like him for Olivia and her stupid plan. I mean, it wouldn't be pretend, because I *do* like him. Anyway, we just talked, and he was so sad and so heartbroken that I just felt sorry for him. Hamilton's a bitch. I guess I've known that for some time, but then, when I talked to Alex, when I heard about the way she treated him, well, it was hard not to see her for what she truly is.

The other reason I'm avoiding everyone is that things seem so different. Hamilton's quiet and cheerless. Zelda's bubbly and perky. Olivia has stopped hanging out with us altogether, and Shelly's throwing a party. She handed out invitations that look like something you'd get for a wedding. I just don't know where I belong anymore.

All I have is a scrapbook full of meaningless pictures. Last night, I took a half-used roll of film from my camera, pulling it out beneath the glow of my desk lamp to destroy every last worthless image on there. Shots of Fidelity's finest having fun, laughing, reveling in the joys of being teenagers. What's that to me? It's all so worthless. I put the camera away.

I'm back to being that clueless freshman girl on the first day of school who's been assigned to the wrong class, only this time there's no Hamilton there to rescue me, to grab me by the hand and steer me in the right direction. I suppose you could say that things are back to the way they should be. I mean for me, anyway. I really never was supposed to be a popular girl. Perhaps I'll make some new friends, some ordinary, boring girls, and we'll do ordinary, boring girl things together. Like the girl who's sitting in front of me right now in history class. Her name's Jennifer. I think she's in the band. We could sleep over at each other's houses. We could go nail polish shopping. But somehow the thought of these normal pastimes makes me want to gag. I wish everything could go back to being the way it used to be.

When I catch a glimpse of blond hair passing by the

classroom doorway, I do something that isn't ordinary or boring. I get up without asking permission, without getting a pass, and walk right out of class to follow her.

"Hamilton?" I call, and she's so deeply lost in her own world that she doesn't look up at first. I have to call her a second time before she responds.

"Nordica, hey. What are you doing skipping class?"

"I saw you go by," I say. "How are you doing?"

"Okay," she says, but then shrugs, and I know she's not okay.

What I said about Hamilton being a bitch is true. I mean, I truly believe it. Only now Hamilton isn't such a bitch; now Hamilton isn't much of anything. She seems to barely exist at all. She's just a pale shadow of her former self. All that spark, all that life that made her who she was is gone or buried somewhere. I know she's crushed about losing Alex, even though she's the one who pushed him away.

Okay, so I feel guilty. I feel like the shittiest friend in the universe. After everything Hamilton did for me, after being such a good friend, after all that, I had to go and betray her trust, and for that I feel totally and completely guilty. I'm not talking about what happened at the party, which like I said was nothing, and even if it had been something, it was after Hamilton and Alex split up anyway, so it wouldn't really have been wrong. I'm talking about way before that, the night of the sleet, when Alex kissed me in his car, when I kissed Alex. I can't help but feel that's what spurred the two of them to split. Maybe

Hamilton found out. Maybe Alex told her. Because otherwise, I don't understand why she would break up with someone that she loves so much.

"Are you going to Shelly's party?" I ask, because I don't know what else to say.

"Yeah, it could be interesting," she says.

"Hamilton?"

"Yes, Nordica."

"I'm sorry."

"For what?"

"Alex. The party. Olivia."

"That's nothing," she says. "Don't worry about it. Speaking of Olivia, you haven't seen her, have you?" I shake my head. "Yeah, neither have I. You better get back to class before you get in trouble."

I nod and start to obediently walk back to history, looking over my shoulder once at the girl who used to be Hamilton Best. I think of that terrifying first day of school, and I see my own pathetic self in the slump of Hamilton's shoulders, in the listless way she walks down the hallway. Hamilton doesn't need some stupid apology. What she needs is my help. I feel completely unqualified, but I don't let that stop me.

"This is all wrong," I say.

"Skipping class?"

"No. You, moping around. Hamilton Best doesn't mope."

"You wouldn't understand."

"I wouldn't understand? Hamilton, I think I could teach

you a thing or two about moping." This, at least, gets a smile out of her, but she shakes her head.

"It's no use. It's all going to come to an end soon. Graduation."

"Well, then, we'll just have to figure out a way around that, won't we?" I say.

She looks at me hopefully, and I feel like that amazing goddess of a girl who single-handedly rearranged my schedule freshman year and made me into one of the most popular girls in the school. I feel empowered. It feels good.

zelda

Because yesterday the lipstick countdown read *73 DAYS UNTIL PROM*, because I should have known better than to count on Shelly Trust to handle anything, because I know deep down that the best way to get something done is to do it oneself, I've decided to make sure that Alex Journer is my prom date. I haven't spent the past three and a half years totally lost in an apathetic haze, despite what some people might think. I've been observant, and I've learned a thing or two from Hamilton in that time, and one of the things I've learned is that one has to be bold and that it doesn't hurt to have a flair for the dramatic. Shelly said she would talk to Alex and use her skills of gentle persuasion to finesse him into asking me to the prom, but given that the lipstick countdown says 73 days, we've moved way beyond gentle persuasion. Desperate times call for desperate measures.

I bought my dress two weeks ago. It took me that long to find it, but finding the perfect prom dress is a lot of work. There's so many things to be taken into consideration: color, length, style, do they have it in your size? My dress is a deep purple with spaghetti straps, a cleavage-bearing neckline, and ruffles from ass to toe. It looks stunning on me. In fact, I look so good in the dress that I know when Alex takes one look at me in it, he will have no choice but to agree to take me to the prom. That's why I wear it to school.

I step in the front doors of school and all eyes are on me. The denim jacket I threw on to keep warm doesn't exactly match the purple taffeta and doesn't exactly do much to disguise the gown beneath, but I hug it to me as if it's a life vest keeping me afloat. With each step, my confidence grows just a little bit more. I take advantage of my audience and parade down the hallway like a model down a runway, knowing that I look just as breathtaking as any catwalk cutie.

My target is standing at his locker, perhaps the only one in the entire hallway who hasn't turned to look at me. Well, that's typical Alex, lost in his own world, oblivious to the world around him. Only when I'm a few feet away does he pick up on the sudden hush that's descended upon the crowded hallway, or the fact that everyone seems to be staring at something just behind him. He turns to look and his sad eyes light up with surprise, perhaps even a dash of happiness.

"I think you might be overdressed," he says.

"It's my prom dress. I was worried I wouldn't have another chance to get to wear it. You see, I don't have a date yet, and, well, there's only one guy I would really want to go with anyway."

"I'm not sure..." He doesn't finish. I don't know what he was planning on saying, but I see his brow wrinkle in confusion.

"Alex, I know you haven't exactly gotten over Hamilton, but did you ever think it might be fated to happen this way?"

"Fate?" he asks, still looking confused. He glances around the hallway. Everyone is staring at us. He's clearly uncomfortable, but I know it's better this way. He has to give me an answer, and how can he turn me down in front of all these people?

"Think about it," I say. "We're like soul mates. We're so much alike, you and I, both outsiders who've never quite fit in. It was Hamilton that brought us together. It was like it was meant to be, all along."

"Zelda? What?" he sputters, unable to get out even a single sentence. I have to admit, I'm getting nervous. I at least expected Alex to be semi-lucid, but it's like he drank half a bottle of NyQuil before going to bed and I'm now trying to wake him up in the middle of the night. "You want to go to the prom? You want to go to the prom with me?" he finally says.

"Is that so crazy?"

"Crazy? Look, Zelda, I'm just not sure... Why don't we talk about this later?"

"I need an answer, Alex."

"You're not acting like yourself."

"What's that supposed to mean?"

"You're Zelda, right? You're not supposed to care about the prom. You don't wear frilly dresses."

His words make me feel dizzy. I just want to go somewhere and lie down. I start to run down the hallway.

"Wait!" Alex cries. I don't stop. Then he yells, "Hamilton!" and I run faster.

Of course, she would pick this moment to show up, and what does she think of me, pathetic and rejected in my perfect dress, running down the hallway as everyone stares after me. I run right back out the doors, hoping the cool air will revive me, or at least freeze any tears that want so desperately to fall.

I try not to think about what's just happened. But I can't get the image of Alex out of my mind, his surprise and confusion, then the way he got so upset with me. That's what hurt the worst—his claim that I wasn't acting the way I was supposed to act, like there was some list of rules somewhere that said I had to do this and say that and wear whatever. I suppose those rules also say that Zelda isn't supposed to get the man, that no matter how much she wants him, the Alex Journers of this world will never be hers.

I look back at the doors, willing Alex to step outside, but the doors remain closed. Alex is not going to come for me. He's probably right at this moment laughing about me with Hamilton, no doubt holding her in his arms. They're probably making up as I sit here shivering in the cold, all alone.

Well, not entirely alone. Jasmine runs up the sidewalk as if a pack of rabid wolves are nipping at her heels. She's dressed in one of her usual eccentric outfits; this one includes a hat with a giant sunflower on it, but truth be told, my own outfit puts hers to shame in terms of its eccentricity.

"Whew," she says when she sees me. "I thought I was late."

"You are," I say.

"What are you doing out here? Aren't you going in?"

"I've had a rough morning."

"Cool dress," she says.

"It was supposed to be my prom dress."

"It's very pretty."

"But it looks as if I won't get a chance to wear it."

"How come?"

"I asked Alex to go to the prom with me, but he didn't seem so keen on the idea."

"Didn't you guys break up?"

"What are you talking about?" I say. "I wasn't dating Alex. He was Hamilton's boyfriend."

She looks at me with that same confused look I saw on Alex's face. It almost makes me feel a little bit better. Here is someone who knows even less than I do about high school politics and romances and such.

"Are you okay, Hamilton?" she asks. "You look kind of pale."

I look behind me, but there's no one there. It's just the two of us.

"I'm Zelda," I say. Is this girl really so dense that all this time, she's thought I was Hamilton?

"Zelda?" she asks. "What is that, like, your alter ego? I like it. It's very funky, very mysterious."

"My name is Zelda," I try to explain, but the confusion on her face isn't going away.

Then a green station wagon with a dented back fender pulls up to the curb and the window rolls down, revealing a frazzled-looking middle-aged woman at the wheel.

"Janey?" she calls. A vice grip tightens on my head. I feel so lightheaded, I'm afraid I might pass out. Jasmine looks at me curiously, like maybe I've suddenly sprouted a second head. "Janey?" the woman repeats. "Is this your friend? I'm glad to see you with a friend, sweetie. It's good for you. You should invite her over sometime."

"Is Janey your real name?" Jasmine asks.

I can do nothing more than shake my head. It hurts so bad.

"Janey? Are you all right? Sweetie, Alex called me. He was worried about you."

"Please," I say, but my voice is only a whisper. I'm too weak to speak any louder. "I'm Zelda," I say, in a voice so faint I don't think it can be heard. "I'm Zelda."

I grasp wildly for some piece of reality to hold on to, but it all seems to be slipping past so fast.

Part Two

ALex

1

I can't shake the image of her, in that dress, from my head. She looked breathtaking, stunning. I'm an idiot, a complete and total idiot. I should have just agreed to go to the prom with her. If I had, maybe it would have all worked itself out somehow. Could that have been enough to bring things back to normal, or what passed for normal in Hamilton's world?

She startled me. The whole thing was so bizarre, I didn't know what to say. I shouldn't have said anything. If I had just kept my mouth shut, it would have been okay, but maybe I've kept my mouth shut for too long. Maybe that's the problem.

Still, I can't help feeling like the biggest chicken on the planet. A braver person would have been there for her. A braver person wouldn't have called someone else to step in and handle things for him. I know that I've failed her. I hate myself.

Locked away in my bedroom, I replay the morning's events again and again in my head. I see her walking away from me a hundred times, a thousand times. I see the hurt look on her beautiful face, and it's like someone's stabbing a knife into my heart. As if these weeks haven't been torture enough, I've now brought more upon myself. Stupid, stupid, stupid.

The phone rings and my stomach cramps up. Without looking at it, I know it's her. No, she wouldn't call me. Why the hell would she want to talk to me? But, still, maybe it's her. It could be. What if it is? Damn it, what do I say to her if it is? I wish I knew what to say to make things all right, to make things like they used to be. No, that's not it. Things were never really all right. I know that better than anyone. I think, maybe, I'm the only one who knows.

I answer the phone. I just want to hear her voice. I want her to know I never meant to hurt her.

"Alex?" Her voice is so faint and weak. She sounds a million miles away.

"How are you doing?" I ask.

"Oh, well, the usual, I guess."

"I miss you. I'm sorry."

She doesn't say anything, but she makes a noise on the other end. She might be crying. I can't tell.

"I have this scrapbook," she says. "It has all these pictures of kids from school. I used to think if I looked at these pictures long enough, I would finally understand it. Like, I don't know, like there's some sort of Periodic Table of Popularity and there's some sort of scientific law that governs the whole thing, but now I realize I was completely mistaken."

"If they awarded Nobel prizes in high school popularity, you would be a shoe-in." I think this will please her, but, of course, I'm completely mistaken.

"I'm serious. Don't joke. Alex, do you remember the night of the Halloween party? You said I should just be myself."

"That's what I told Nordica," I say.

The line goes silent for a second or two, long enough to make me wonder if the call got dropped.

"This is Nordica," she says.

Crap. Of course it is. I am an idiot. She even sounded like Nordica, with her faint and trembling voice, but I was so desperate for Hamilton that I heard what I wanted to hear. Well, these past few weeks things have gotten so weird, with Hamilton acting less and less like Hamilton. The scrapbook, though; it was Nordica who kept the scrapbook. I knew that. What's wrong with me?

"Nordica. Sorry. I thought you were Hamilton. It's just that I haven't talked to her in a while. You couldn't maybe put her on?"

"She's not here."

"No, of course not. Sorry."

More silence. This time longer than the first, long enough for me to get my hopes up.

"I've figured it all out," she says.

"Popularity?"

"How to fix everything." She sounds so serious. Her voice is cool and confident and completely un-Nordica-like.

"Oh. Do you mean with us?"

"It's like that first day of school, when Hamilton fixed my schedule. Hamilton's scared to death of her graduation, and so am I. I figured out how to fix that, how to get out of it."

"I've told you before, failing English is not that easy."

She laughs at this. It's a relief from the deadly seriousness. She sounds a little bit like the Nordica I know.

"Failing English would just postpone the inevitable," she says. There's a noise on the other end. It could be a sigh. It could be her closing the cover on her scrapbook.

"So, what?" I ask. "You're going to drop out?"

"In a matter of speaking. This world is too much for me. It's time to move on."

I'm not exactly sure what she's saying, but I have enough sense to panic.

"What world?" I ask. I can't get the question out fast enough. "The world of high school?"

"The world in general," Nordica says. "I don't think I was ever meant to be here."

"That's not true. Hamilton needs you." Scary images race through my mind at a furious pace. I see Hamilton lying in her bathtub, blood pouring from her slit wrists. I see her with a gun in her mouth, pulling the trigger to end it all with one loud ugly bang. But I'm talking to Nordica, and that's not the way Nordica would check out, if she even has the nerve to do it at all. She could just be talking hypothetically.

"I know. I'm doing this for Hamilton."

"You need to think about this."

"I have thought about it. It makes perfect sense."

"Of course." I backpedal. A cool nervous sweat has broken out on my forehead. If only I could find the exact right words. What are you supposed to say to someone who is contemplating suicide? Why don't they ever teach us anything useful in school?

"Alex, you've always been nice to me," she says. The words are like a new dagger to my heart. This one has a serrated edge. I have to remind myself that this is Nordica, that she doesn't know any better. "I just wanted to call to say goodbye."

"No, wait!" My voice breaks in my panicked shout. "What do you mean goodbye? What do you mean?"

"I can't keep doing this. I need to be myself. I don't belong here."

"Then go somewhere you belong."

"I'm stuck here. I got a whole 'nother year of this hell, and I just can't do it anymore. I can't stand it another day."

"I won't let you do this."

"Look, I don't want you to think this is your fault. Probably the only reason I didn't check out sooner is because of you, but this is what I need to do, and I hope you can understand and accept that."

"I can't and I won't. Nordica, listen to me. What are you planning to do?" I feel like I have to keep her talking. Nordica listens to me. She values my opinion. All I need to do is find the magic words, and if I can keep her on the line long enough, maybe I can do that.

"I don't belong in this world."

"Nordica, you can always just leave. Like Olivia. You can just, you know, disappear. Do you understand? Do you understand?"

"Goodbye, Alex."

This time I know the silence on the other end is real. My heart is pounding. I don't know what to do. This is all my fault. I hate myself. I want to find myself a hole in the ground somewhere and crawl in and just cry for my poor pathetic self, but first things first. For the second time that day I make a phone call to a woman who hates my guts. Well, on that subject, we're on the same page.

2

It would be a lie to say I'd never considered the possibility that Hamilton Best might fall for me. I've always been something of a dreamer, and really, was there a straight guy at Fidelity who hadn't had at least one fantasy involving Hamilton? So, I'd considered the possibility, but I knew that realistically I didn't have a chance with the most popular girl in the school. I didn't see much point in torturing myself dreaming about a girl who didn't know I existed. So, I pretty much put her out of my mind, as much as anyone could put Hamilton Best out of their mind.

I used to think it was fate that brought me and Hamilton together, but if it was fate, it was the sort of fate that Hamilton manipulated to her own ends. It was early fall of our junior year, and it had been pouring rain all day. I didn't live far from the school, and lacking both a car and the license needed to legally drive it, I was stuck walking. When the weather was nice it was fine. When it was pouring, it sucked. That day, I pulled my hood up over me and started up the paved path that led from school back to the housing development where I lived.

I saw something up ahead on the path, but couldn't quite tell what it was. Was it trash? Had someone dropped their jacket? I got a little bit closer and realized it wasn't something, but someone. I broke into a jog, and when I was a few feet away, I realized it was Hamilton. I don't think I'd ever spoken a word to the queen of popularity, and ordinarily I wouldn't have known how to speak to her without my tongue getting tied up in knots, but when I saw her lying there, there was no time to worry about social anxiety.

"Hamilton!" I called. "Are you all right?"

She was lying on her side on the ground in an awkward position, but when she heard me she looked up and smiled at me.

"Alex," she said. "Thank God you're here."

I was trying to stay focused on the moment, but it wasn't easy when a little voice inside my head was shouting, *She knows my name! She knows my name!*

"What happened?" I asked.

"I slipped. It's these stupid shoes, they're completely impractical. I think I twisted my ankle."

I leaned down and offered her my hand. She took it. I was so glad it was raining, otherwise my hand would have been soaked with nervous sweat. I helped her to her feet.

She attempted to put some weight on her injured ankle and immediately tottered, as if she was about to fall. I caught her, and she threw her arm around my neck, leaning her weight against me. I wished I'd tried a bit harder to make some friends in school; I felt an overwhelming need to run and tell someone about this, not that anyone would believe it.

"I feel like such a spaz," Hamilton said.

"You're not a spaz," I said. I didn't ever want this moment to end, and I knew that what I was supposed to do was charm her with some witty conversation, but my brain had turned to mush. "Um, I can walk you back to the school, if you want."

"That would be great," she said. She smiled, and right then the heavens opened up and the heavy rain turned into torrential rain.

We started back toward the school, but it was going to take us forever with her hobbling along.

"Hang on," I said. I'm a long way from being muscle-bound, and I wasn't sure if I would be able to carry Hamilton without collapsing like a weakling, but I remember reading somewhere about how in an emergency, adrenaline kicks in and allows people to perform feats of strength that would normally be beyond them. I hoped that this was one of those moments. I hoisted Hamilton up into my arms. It took every last ounce of strength I had, but, like a chivalrous knight, I carried her the whole way back to the school.

I'm not going to lie. I'm not generally superficial, but that afternoon I prayed my fellow students were watching as I performed my hero act for the most popular girl at Fidelity.

By the time we stepped inside the school, my arms felt like Jell-O and we were both completely drenched. I carefully lowered Hamilton to the floor, my arms still around her as she balanced on her good ankle. I didn't want to let go of her, and she made no move to step away from me. My heart was racing, and that was only partly due to my excessive physical exertion.

"Thanks," she said. Her voice was soft and sweet. She looked up at me, and even though she was drenched, her hair hanging limp and wet and dripping onto the floor, streaks of makeup running down her face, she was still beautiful.

I knew I shouldn't overstay my welcome. I knew that I should accept her gratitude and be on my way, let us both get back to our separate worlds. Only I couldn't move. In the past few seconds, I'd grown roots and seemed to be firmly planted in the hallway's floor.

"Well, um, I should . . ." I stammered, but I never finished what I was going to say, if I'd even known in the first place. Hamilton was looking at me, and I knew I'd never have an opportunity like this again. But it certainly wasn't a rational decision on my part; I was no longer capable of rational thought. I bent down and kissed her gently on her lips. She didn't push me away. Instead she leaned into me and kissed me back.

And like that it happened. Fate in the form of a rainstorm and a slippery pair of shoes had transformed my entire life, or so I thought at the time. Of course, now I wonder if Hamilton really fell, if her ankle really was hurt, or if that was some carefully calculated plot to bring the two of us together.

3

I hang up the phone and begin to pace my room like a caged rat. I can't stay here. I'll go crazy, too, if I do. I grab my car keys and run down the stairs, taking them two at a time.

"Is everything all right?" my mother asks. She's in the kitchen cooking dinner. Nothing is remotely all right, but there's no way to explain this to her.

"Yeah," I say. "I just need to go out for a bit." Her face falls. I don't share a lot of personal details with my parents. I mean, they know I was dating Hamilton, and they've met her and think she's a nice girl, but that's about it.

"What about dinner?" she asks.

"I'm not really feeling that hungry."

She nods, and I can tell she knows something is wrong, but she doesn't say anything. She goes back to stirring a pot on the stove and I make my escape.

I pull up in front of Hamilton's house. No one is home. Are they at the hospital? All the lights are off. I sit in my car, staring at the house I've spent so much time in. I think of all the parties I've attended here. The dark and empty house bears little resemblance to the way it looks when one of Hamilton's parties is in full swing. As much as I hated those parties, it makes me sad to think that there may never be another one.

Where is she? Will Mrs. Best call and let me know what's going on? Do I even deserve a phone call? No, I don't.

I drive over to the school. The student parking lot is mostly deserted at this hour, and I'm grateful. I pull into a dark corner of the lot and kill the engine. I sit there and stare up at the school, Hamilton's castle.

I wish I had someone to talk to. I wish Olivia was here. She'd listen to me. She'd be honest with me. She would have no compunction about telling me what a complete and total dickhead I am. God, I miss her, and just missing her is proof that I'm a despicable human being.

4

Guys like me do not date girls like Hamilton Best. It doesn't happen. Not in a million years. The Hamilton Bests of the world can have any guy they want. That's how it works. So, when you're a guy like me and a girl like Hamilton says she wants you, well, you just figure that in some past life you must have done something like rescue a bunch of kids from a burning building, or saved your platoon by throwing yourself on a grenade or something like that, and you say that you are hers and you follow her around like the pathetically loyal dog you are. I think I spent the first six months of our relationship in a state of near shock, sure that at any moment I would wake up and realize the whole thing was only a dream. Then I did wake up, and realized it was something else entirely.

My girlfriend, the flawless Hamilton Best, turned out to be not so flawless after all. The most popular girl in school had issues that went way beyond your average personality quirk. The clinical term for it, I've learned, is dissociative identity disorder, which is a fancy way of saying she shared her brain with four other personalities. It was sort of like a buy-one-get-four-free deal. Which would have been nice if I was shopping for a new pair of jeans, but sucked when all I had wanted was a girlfriend.

When I first started dating Hamilton, I was infatuated with her. I adored her. I thought about her constantly. She may have been my reason for living. I'm not sure. What I am sure of is that I was not in love with her, not at first; I didn't know her well enough to be in love with her. I was awestruck. I was a gawky dork, a loner, a loser, and I was dating the hands-down most beautiful, most popular girl in the school. I was so overwhelmed by the whole thing that I couldn't even begin to become emotionally involved.

The weird thing was, nothing in my life changed when I started dating Hamilton Best. I mean, suddenly I had this beautiful girl to hang out with after school or to take to the movies on the weekend, true, and I did get yelled at by my parents on more than one occasion for spending too much time on the phone, but it wasn't like who I was suddenly changed. I didn't suddenly become this cool, popular guy. I was still a dork who pretty much kept to himself. I just happened to be the dork who was Hamilton's boyfriend.

I am an optimistic person. In my pre-Hamilton days, I always sort of figured that life was waiting for me right around the corner, that one morning I would wake up and suddenly I'd have it all, the sort of life I'd always imagined. The sort of life where I was cool, the guy everyone wanted to be friends with. I hungered for social acceptance.

Kissing Hamilton that rainy afternoon changed everything, and at the same time it changed nothing. It's not like I suddenly became a different person.

In fact, I proved it the very next day, when I met Hamilton at her locker to ask how her ankle was and instead blurted out, "So are we, well, what I'm saying is, would you maybe want to hang out sometime? With me, I mean." I could feel the stares of our classmates as they wondered what someone like me was doing talking to the queen herself. I was ready for her to laugh in my face and tell me to go to hell.

"Yeah, Alex, I do," Hamilton said.

"Really?" I asked like a complete idiot. "That's awesome!"

"I need a man in my life," Hamilton said. She smiled at me. I couldn't remember how to breathe. "This doesn't mean I'm going to eat lunch with you, though." She smiled again and I wondered if it was a joke, but she didn't laugh. Social misfit that I was, I still knew all about Hamilton's lunch table policy. She had her own table, and just like with her guest lists, she decided who was and was not worthy to be a lunch companion on any given day. Some days no one made the cut and she ate alone, looking a bit like a queen on a dais.

"Of course not," I said, trying for a light tone in case she was just joking. She didn't correct me. I decided then and there that I would refrain from eating lunch ever again to spare myself from the awkwardness of figuring out whether I was or was not allowed to eat lunch with Hamilton. It was a small price to pay. I think if she'd requested it, I might have hacked off a limb just for the privilege of being her boyfriend.

Anyway, I figured this was it. The life I'd always dreamed would be mine was finally starting to happen. Hamilton Best had decided that I was her boyfriend, and I assumed this was the beginning of my meteoric rise to high school happiness. Except, of course, I went nowhere. I mean, it wasn't like I was completely unhappy. I was dating the most beautiful, most popular girl in the school. I had copious amounts of happiness, but it was also a dose of reality. If even Hamilton Best couldn't make me a cool guy, then I pretty much had to accept the fact that I was never going to be one.

I'd like to say I took it all in stride, but that's a complete and total load of bullshit. I was afraid to breathe for fear of losing the one decent thing that ever happened in my social life. It all seemed like such a fluke. I was sure that Hamilton would catch on to the fact that I was a complete loser, and I never once considered whether it was my total lack of confidence that had made me so attractive to her in the first place. If you were Hamilton Best and you were hunting for the guy least likely to screw up everything that you'd worked so hard to attain, then you would probably pick someone just like me.

One afternoon the phone rang. My mother grabbed it before I could.

"It's for you!" she shouted from downstairs. "It's that girl again!"

Only it wasn't, not exactly. I took the phone in my bedroom. I shut the door.

"Hey," I said.

"Hey," she said. Even in that one word, I could tell there was something off about her voice. I'm not sure anyone else would have noticed it, but I'd spent a lot of time with Hamilton by then. I thought I knew her inside and outside, backwards and forwards.

I was wrong.

5

With flowers and balloons in hand, I get as far as the receptionist's desk.

"Only family is allowed to visit," the woman on duty says.

"I'm her boyfriend."

"Aw, how sweet, but sorry, no."

"I'm the reason she's not dead," I say. Even I realize that I'm pushing it too far.

"Family only. Young man, if you don't leave, I'll call security to escort you out."

Nordica had overdosed on the low-dose aspirin pills her mother took for her heart. It seemed she couldn't even get that right. She apparently was under the impression that she was taking something far more potent, either that or she didn't really have a death wish. After all, if she really wanted to die, she wouldn't have called me. She would have written a note.

After they purged her system of the low-strength aspirin, they kept her at the hospital for observation. In the morning, she'd be moved to the psychiatric ward. My only experience of such places is what I've seen in movies. I picture drugged-out zombies, homicidal nurses, and frightening experimental treatments. She doesn't belong in a place like that. I mean, she has her problems, but who doesn't? The thing is, if she's been able to get by in the world for so long, she can't really be that crazy, can she?

I wish Hamilton was here. She would convince the receptionist to let me up to see her. She's good at those sort of things. I lack her subtle ease, her grace, her power of persuasion. I consider waiting for an opportunity when the receptionist is distracted to sneak into the elevator and head upstairs, but I suspect there will be more minor authority figures up there, ready to thwart me from getting into her room.

I'm about to step out the hospital doors when someone calls my name. Has the receptionist had a change of heart? I turn and see her there, just past the receptionist's station, glowering at me. Hamilton's mom.

"What are you doing here?" she asks.

"Leaving," I tell her. Hamilton's mom never approved of me. I was not good enough for her daughter.

"Just stay the hell away from her. Haven't you done enough damage already?"

"On the contrary, I don't think I'm the one who did the damage."

"Like hell," she says.

I am surprised by how much older her mom looks than when I last saw her only a few months ago. Her face is more tired, and puffier than usual. Maybe she's a better person than I give her credit for, but it's hard for me to see her as anything but a selfish, uncaring monster. There are so many things I'd like to say to her, but what's the point?

"How is she?" I ask. "How's Hamilton?"

"Hamilton," she responds in a mocking voice, "Hamilton. Just ducky, no thanks to you."

I could point out that I was the one who called her. I don't. Clearly she's decided that this whole predicament is my fault. I can't say that I entirely disagree.

In a quieter voice, Hamilton's mom says, "She nearly killed herself."

6

I was sitting on my bed, the phone pressed to my ear. My mom was cooking something downstairs that filled the entire house with the stink of onions.

"What's up, Hamilton?" I said. I was concerned because she didn't sound quite right, but it wasn't like she was crying or screaming or anything.

"It's Olivia," the not-quite-right voice on the other end said.

"Olivia?" I repeated. The name meant nothing to me.

"Olivia," she said again, annoyed. "Hamilton's best friend." She obviously hoped this would jog something. It didn't. "The clique," she said.

She might as well have landed from Mars for all the sense she was making. The thing about Hamilton was that she didn't have a lot of friends, not close friends, anyway. I mean, everyone in the school loved her, and anyone who was anyone claimed her as a friend, but Hamilton was of the benevolent-dictator school of popularity. People worshiped her, and she loved them for it. She was friends with everyone, well, everyone who was anyone anyway, but at the same time no one was her good friend. She didn't have any best friends. All her friends were the say-hi-in-the-hall-way sort of friends. She didn't have any whisper-secrets-in-your-ear friends, and she certainly didn't pal around with anyone named Olivia.

"The clique," I repeated. I was trying to figure out what was going on. Obviously this was Hamilton on the other end. So this had to be, what? Some sort of joke? A game? A test?

"Yes, Alex, the clique. Hamilton's friends. Quit being so dense." She sounded annoyed, but that wasn't all. She sounded so different. It was like she had a cold or had lost her voice cheering at a football game. Her voice was changed, lower, huskier. It was subtle, but I heard it.

"I don't really get it," I said.

"Okay, this is getting annoying," she said.

"Is it a joke?"

"Is what a joke? Alex, forget it. I've got to go."

"Wait," I said, but the line had already gone dead.

I sat there for a while, staring at the phone, trying to make sense of what had just happened. I was still trying to make sense of it when my mom yelled upstairs that dinner was ready.

The next morning I caught up with Hamilton before homeroom. She was so normal, I thought I'd imagined the whole thing yesterday. Maybe I fell asleep and dreamed it all.

"Hey, you called me yesterday," I said.

"No I didn't," she said.

Perhaps it was a dream. "You said your name was Olivia."

Hamilton froze. Her face went pale. "Olivia called you?"

So, not a dream.

"Who's Olivia?" I asked.

"Just someone I know," she said. "What did she say?"

"Not much. Something about some clique. She sounded like you."

"Well, we've known each other a long time."

"You never mentioned her before."

The homeroom bell rang.

"I've got to go," she said.

"Does she go to school here?"

"We've gone to school together since kindergarten."

She ran down the hallway to homeroom. I stared after her. I was even more confused than I'd been the previous afternoon.

7

Coming back to school after New Year's, when I was no longer Alex, Hamilton's boyfriend but simply Alex, was hard enough, but this is worse. Fidelity without Hamilton feels completely and totally wrong. There's a strange stillness, a dark mood that hangs over the entire school. Outside it's sunny and warm, an almost springlike day full of hope and promise, but inside it feels cold and clammy.

I hear whispers everywhere I go. I see little clusters of students huddled together in the hallway as I walk past. They speak in low tones. They look at me, then quickly look away. It's not hard to tell what they're talking about. I wonder what they've heard. I wonder how much they know. They probably hate and blame me as much as Hamilton's mom does.

By third period, I am beginning to wonder if I should

bust into the office, commandeer the PA system, and just make some sort of formal announcement. It would feel great to get things off my chest. I'm not even sure where I'd begin. In order to make them realize I'm not a complete and total jerk, I'd have to go back to the very beginning. It's a long story. I'm pretty sure the principal would pull the plug on me before I got too far. So I suffer in silence.

At lunch I stand against the cafeteria wall staring at her table. It's empty. Everyone avoids it like it's contaminated. They give it a wide berth as they walk past. A kid I don't know comes up to me. He's an underclassmen, just overweight enough to tip me off that he probably isn't part of the in-crowd.

"Hey, Alex," he says, like he knows me. It occurs to me that he may have been at one of Hamilton's parties. All sorts of unusual people started showing up at her parties toward the end there.

"Hey," I say cautiously.

"I just wanted to say, you know, no matter what, I think she's a good person."

"Yeah," I agree. "Thanks."

He doesn't hang around asking questions, pressing me for details. He just walks right back to his table. When I walk past a group of whispering students a few minutes later, his words stay with me. She *is* a good person. I'm not the only one who knows it.

8

So we'd had two completely perplexing conversations about some alleged friend of hers who supposedly went to school with us even though I had no idea who this friend was. Other than that little bit of weirdness, everything was absolutely fine. I'm not the sort of person who has much interest in rocking boats. I decided I would not bring up the Olivia subject.

I didn't, and Hamilton didn't, and for a little while, things seemed to be going pretty well. I almost forgot entirely about those strange conversations. Except, of course, they were a little bit too strange to completely forget. I remembered them in all-too-vivid clarity when I was walking Hamilton home from school one afternoon.

"Shelly's getting on my nerves," Hamilton said.

I'd never really stayed up on the whole Fidelity High social scene, so at first I just assumed Shelly was some girl at school. I thought she might be that curly-haired girl in my history class that I saw Hamilton eating lunch with last week.

"Why's that?" I asked.

"She's a stuck-up, pushy know-it-all," Hamilton said.

"Well, that would get on my nerves, too."

"I know. At lunch today she told Olivia to go to hell, and then told me, in front of everyone, that Olivia had no business being in the clique."

I kept walking, because instinctively I knew I had to pretend to be on the same page as Hamilton. But each step was that much harder to take, like my feet were suddenly encased in cement blocks. I'd seen Hamilton at lunch. She was eating alone.

"Is Shelly part of the clique?" I asked, my voice nearly cracking, even though what I wanted to ask was who these mysterious people were. Were they some sort of weird high school version of imaginary friends?

"Against my own better judgment, she is," Hamilton said. "She can be so irritating."

She stopped suddenly. When I turned toward her, her face was deadly serious.

"Listen. I'm telling you all this in confidence, because I trust you, Alex. But you can't ever tell Shelly. You can't tell anyone."

"Of course not."

"Promise me."

"I promise." I had no idea just what I was promising.

9

I keep expecting it to get easier. I don't know why—it never does. Fidelity is only a shadow of its former self without its unofficial queen. Hamilton was the thing that made Fidelity High what it was, and Hamilton was the thing that made me a whole and complete person. Her absence is a big gaping hole that's too difficult to ignore.

I can't get used to life without her. I'll be walking down the hallway and hear, around the corner, the sound of artificial laughter. *Shelly!* I race around the corner only to find a group of girls I don't know. They study me with judgmental eyes.

A camera went off when I was in art class and I spun around, expecting to see Nordica with her beat-up old camera, and it's just some old guy snapping pictures for the school website. I wonder about Nordica's scrapbook. She was looking at it the night she called me, the last time she spoke to me, the last time I spoke to any of them.

As I pull a book out of my locker one afternoon, something tumbles out onto the floor, a piece of paper. I bend down to pick it up. It's an envelope, with my name written on it in Shelly's familiar, bubbly script. My excitement fades quickly when I realize what it is. It's the invitation to her party, the party that will never happen. I didn't read the invitation before. It was easier to ignore it than face the ugliness of reality. Now, as I study it, I realize what a perplexing document this must have been for someone who didn't know Hamilton better; that is, everyone else who received a copy.

The elegant invitation states that the party is being thrown by Shelly Trust. *"Who?"* people must have thought when reading it. Perhaps they thought it was some sort of strange joke by Hamilton, the same thing I thought after my first conversation with Olivia. The invitation says the party will be held at the Trusts' home, but then lists an address that everyone who received an invite would have known was Hamilton's house.

"I never got one of those," says a girl I remember from the parties. I can understand why she didn't get an invitation. She's not Shelly's sort of person.

"Doesn't matter," I say.

"How's she doing?"

"Who?" I snap. I'm tired of people prying.

"Hamilton," she says. I shouldn't have snapped at her.

"I don't know," I say.

"I was her friend," the girl says. Suddenly I know who she is. It's that Jasmine girl. She wasn't on any of the guest lists.

"Hamilton had enough friends," I say. I'm being intentionally mean and I don't care. I want to hurt this girl. It's stupid, but I'm jealous of her and her supposed friendship with Hamilton.

"Yeah, but nobody really knew her."

On that score she's right. Well, almost right. Almost nobody knew her.

10

One morning, I was ditching Spanish class and was surprised to see Hamilton in the hallway, an ancient camera around her neck.

"What are you doing?" I asked.

She blushed and mumbled something. She wouldn't meet my eyes. She was acting so unlike herself, I thought she was mad at me.

"Is something wrong?" I asked.

"What if I fail English? They'll kick me out of school. Everyone will laugh at me."

"Whoa. You're not failing English. And even if you were, nobody gets kicked out of school for failing English. And in case you haven't noticed, nobody laughs at Hamilton."

"I don't know if the courtesy extends to her friends, especially her most pathetic of friends."

A light bulb went off in my head. Even though I was talking to Hamilton, I wasn't really talking to Hamilton. It was like that conversation on the phone.

"Olivia?" I said. Hamilton who wasn't really Hamilton rolled her eyes in response. "Shelly?" I ventured. This earned me a snort of laughter.

"I meant me, Alex," she said.

"You," I repeated, dumbfounded. Then, because I had to say something, I said, "You're not pathetic."

"Even if I fail English?"

"I don't think that's going to happen."

"I turned in my paper a day late."

"Well, speaking from experience, I can say that's not usually grounds for failure."

I caught up with Hamilton on her way into the cafeteria at lunch time. I didn't see the camera and she seemed to be acting like herself, but I wasn't entirely sure.

"How are you?" I asked.

"Fine," she said. She looked at me as if maybe I was a little bit crazy. I didn't care because at least I knew it was her, Hamilton.

Well, the girl I thought of as Hamilton. I didn't really have any model for what I was dealing with. In my mind she was kind of like a superhero. I thought of meek and mild Clark Kent who could suddenly become the dashing and daring Superman, or Bruce Wayne, who at the first sign of trouble transformed into Batman. Clark Kent and Superman were the same person, but not really. Hamilton was like that, except without the cape and the fighting crime and all. I wondered who the real Hamilton was. Maybe the awkward, nervous girl I'd run into in the hallway was the real Hamilton, and this cool, confident popular girl was just a cover. It was weird and insane and completely terrifying.

Except this was high school, and we were all playing parts. Trying to be something you're not is pretty much the whole point of high school. I tried telling myself that Hamilton wasn't different than anyone else I went to school with except for the fact that she was more accomplished at playing these roles, but I knew there was more to it than that. It wasn't like she was playing a role. It was like she actually became these other girls.

"Hey, who's your friend with the camera?" I asked.

"Nordica," she said, in that same have-you-lost-your-mind tone.

"Nordica, right," I repeated. "I ran into her earlier. Couldn't remember her name."

"You're pathetic," she said. The word choice was haunting. I waited, but I saw no flicker of recognition on her face. She had no memory of our earlier conversation. She shook her head in a what-am-I-going-to-do-with-you sort of way.

I waited, hoping that maybe today she'd ask me to join her at the hallowed lunch table, but she said nothing else and headed off to buy her lunch. I was her boyfriend. I know I shouldn't have needed the validation of a lunch table invite, but it hurt me all the same.

I watched her as she carried her tray back to her table. Today she hadn't invited anyone else to join her, either. I watched her eat her lunch alone. At least, I'd always assumed she was alone. Now, I wasn't so sure.

My head was spinning. On the one hand, I was dating the most beautiful girl in the school. On the other hand, she was completely insane. I looked around the crowded cafeteria. They all adored Hamilton. For a moment, I wondered if I was the last one to know.

I recalled the deadly serious look in her eyes that day I walked her home. She'd confided a secret in me, ostensibly a secret about how she felt about one of her friends. It was the sort of secret that gets confided at any high school, anywhere, but really, that wasn't Hamilton's secret at all. Her real secret was monstrously huge—and she had entrusted it to me.

As I watched her sitting there all alone, but not really all alone, the enormous burden of that secret weighed down on me.

11

It's not as if life without Hamilton has suddenly turned me into this apathetic, horrible student, but it certainly hasn't improved my previously less-than-stellar academic performance. If you miss enough days, they'll bar you from graduating. So I force myself to get out of bed each morning. But since being late for school earns you no worse than the occasional day spent in detention, I force myself out of bed each morning but not necessarily on time. When they see me walk into the main office, they don't have to ask what I want. They just start filling out the late pass.

Today, though, the secretary is on the phone when I walk in. As I wait, I listen to her side of the conversation. It doesn't mean anything to me at first.

Not until I hear her say, "She's such a sweet girl. Everyone loves her. It would be a shame for her not to graduate just because of something like this."

My ears prick up. I find myself leaning across the counter, straining to hear every word.

"No reason we can't send her assignments over there. Bernedorn? How do you spell that? I'm sure we can work something out as far as her final exams are concerned." She jots down something on a piece of paper. I'm too far away to make out details, but it has the look of an address. "Well, you take care, Mrs. Best."

The secretary looks a bit flustered when she hangs up. It's a few seconds before she looks up. When she does, she gives me a crooked smile.

"I suppose you'll be wanting a late pass," she says. I nod.

"Is she in a mental institution?" I ask.

"I can't really say," she says. She begins to fill out my late pass. She hands it to me, but I don't leave.

"I just want to know if she's all right," I say.

"She apparently had some serious problems," the secretary says with a sigh. "You wouldn't have known it to look at her."

12

As long as Hamilton never got too close to anyone, her secret was safe. She was smart, smooth, and cool, and an inherently likable person—not in spite of her psychological problems but because of them. I knew this better than anyone.

It didn't take me long to realize that there were certain subtle clues to let me know who she was. If she was acting weird and moody, she was Zelda. When she was droll and cynical, she was Olivia. If she was overly concerned with what other people were wearing, she was Shelly. If she seemed shy and nervous, she was Nordica. There also were slight changes in the cadence of her voice that would tip me off. Sometimes I could tell by who she selected to eat lunch with her that day, or who she chatted with in the hallway. I became adept at detecting the different ways she walked depending on who she was.

Soon, I knew her. I knew all of her, and so, naturally, I fell completely and totally in love with her.

In general, people can be pretty boring. That's not politically correct to say, but it's true. It's like if you're dating this girl, and, I don't know, she's in the color guard, and maybe she collects Pez dispensers, and when she grows up she wants to become a veterinarian or something. So pretty soon, you know everything there is to know about this girl. I mean, she can be cute and funny and all, but after a while you're going to get bored. You're going to wonder if maybe there's someone else out there who is cuter and funnier, or maybe not cuter and funnier but just different. Boredom's the number one killer of relationships. Maybe true love is simply finding that one person who never stops being interesting to you.

For me, that person is Hamilton. Well, no, that's not quite right. I loved Hamilton, but I loved the clique as well. Hamilton wasn't really Hamilton without the clique. I know she was seriously messed up, but it didn't seem to hurt her any. She had her shit together—it wasn't like I was taking advantage of some mentally challenged girl or something. I was dating a girl who had turned some serious personality flaws into assets.

It was what made her who she was. It was what made her so popular. Nobody else knew; nobody else really understood what it was about Hamilton that made her so special. They only knew her as Hamilton, but they didn't *only* know Hamilton.

One guest list afternoon, I was walking down a hallway when I heard Olivia talking to another girl in our class. I froze. I thought that this was the end—I thought this other girl would realize that the most popular girl in the school was a complete and total freak. By the following morning, the news would spread through the entire school. Hamilton would be devastated.

I had no plan but I ran toward the pair, prepared to do anything I had to in order to save the love of my life. I threw my arm around her, and Olivia promptly pushed me away.

"Alex," she said, annoyed, "what are you doing?"

The other girl just smiled at us. "Maybe I ought to leave you two in private," she said.

That's when I realized that the girl didn't know. What was so obvious to me—the different voice, the attitude, the posture—was completely undetectable to Hamilton's friends and acquaintances at school. As far as they knew, it was Hamilton. How many times had someone been talking to a member of the clique while not realizing they weren't talking to Hamilton at all? It probably happened all the time.

To her teachers, she was Hamilton. It was the name in their gradebook. It was the name at the top of every assignment she handed in, but I knew it was not necessarily Hamilton completing all those assignments. Couldn't her teachers tell? Did they simply assume she was the most erratic student on the planet? Perhaps they figured she was a cheater, that she bought her papers off the Internet. Whatever the case, they never seemed to mind. Perhaps her teachers, like everyone else, had fallen under her spell.

She was popular, basically, because she wasn't just one thing. She was smart and cool and powerful, but she was also petty and superficial, ordinary and nervous, independent and cynical, different and disaffected. She was a chameleon of a girl. They loved her for it, and so did I.

I was also scared out of my mind. Hamilton had handed me a secret too big for me to handle. I knew I had two options. The first was to seek help; I could have gone to the school nurse, the school psychologist, a teacher, anyone. I could have told them that Hamilton Best, that most universally loved student—cool, calm Hamilton Best, who more than anyone seemed to have it all together—was, in fact, seriously disturbed. After they'd finished laughing at me, chastising me for making up such a ridiculous tale, after all that, *and* if I was able to convince them that what I said was true ... what then? Well, the most popular girl in the school, the girl who lived for the adoration of others, would become, overnight, a complete laughingstock. She would be crushed. I would wound the girl I loved in an irreparable way. But worse than that, I would have violated her trust. I would, inevitably, lose her forever.

Then there was option two. I could keep Hamilton's secret. I could protect the girl whose strong, powerful personality masked her complete fragility. I could do everything in my power to make sure her secret remained hidden. I think she knew, when she chose me to be her boyfriend, that I was the sort of guy who would keep her secret safe. Who would do everything in my power to protect her and make sure I never lost her.

13

I always look over at Hamilton's empty table when I step into the cafeteria. But today, it's not empty. Jasmine is sitting there. I walk over and sit down across from her.

"What are you doing here?" I ask.

"When I started school here in September, I didn't know anyone. It's not easy to change schools when you're a senior."

Shelly did it when she was a sophomore, I think to myself, but then I remember that Shelly isn't a real person.

"I walked into the cafeteria on my first day," Jasmine continues, "and I had no idea where to sit, then I saw this girl sitting all by herself. I went over to sit down, but she told me the seat was taken."

Probably Shelly, I say to myself.

"The thing is, she sat there alone through that whole lunch period. And then on other days, I noticed she ate all alone, and it seemed kind of weird." I hear the hint of an accusation in her voice. I'm not sure what she's driving at.

"Do you think they all hate me?" I ask.

"You mean because you broke up with her?"

"I didn't break up with her," I say, but that's how Hamilton took it. So I guess maybe I did break up with her.

"I was scared," I tell Jasmine. "I didn't know what to do anymore."

14

The parties were always the worst. The five of them would be at each other's throats. Everyone wanted to be part of the action. I couldn't really blame them, since this was pretty much the highlight of being the most popular girl in the school. I'm not sure when I got the brilliant idea to fortify myself with alcohol before the dreaded events, but it quickly became a habit I couldn't break.

It was hard to keep track of who she was throughout the evening, and I think sometimes she got tripped up. I figured if she was ever going to blow her cover, it was going to be at a party. I watched her like a hawk and tried to keep her removed from the action. Of course, this was easier when she was Hamilton, more difficult when she was one of the other girls. By the end of those parties, I was always exhausted. I felt ready to crawl into bed and sleep for days.

After last spring's end-of-the-school-year party, I was hanging out with Hamilton in her kitchen. Everyone else had gone home. She was cleaning things up while I sat at the kitchen table fighting to stay awake.

"It's hard to believe junior year is over already," she said. "Before we know it, we'll be graduating."

"Thank God," I said.

"Why would you say that?" Hamilton said in a sharp, angry tone. I looked up to find her staring at me, her expression hurt. I mentally reviewed what I'd said, to see if I had somehow uttered something horrible. I was pretty sure I hadn't.

"What?" I asked.

"Graduation," she said in a quiet voice. "That's the end of everything."

"Well, I wouldn't put it like that," I mumbled, but I began to understand what she was saying. For someone like Hamilton, for someone who was the reigning champion of this game some called high school, graduation would feel more like the end of something than the start of the rest of our lives. Some of us were looking forward to that day, looking forward to adulthood and all the promises it offered, but Hamilton wasn't one of those people. She had things pretty well under control right now; why would she want that to change? I was an idiot for not realizing just what graduation would mean for someone like Hamilton. Hell, I should have been as scared as she was about that date looming on the horizon.

Then I saw the headlights in the driveway. Hamilton saw them too.

"Damn. My mother," she said. She glanced at the clock: two a.m. "She's early."

"Maybe I should make like a tree," I said, but I didn't move fast enough.

"What are you doing here?" Hamilton's mom said when she saw me. She turned to Hamilton. "I thought I told you I didn't want him here."

"Relax," Hamilton said. "We were just hanging out."

It was a testament to Hamilton's cleaning prowess that upwards of a hundred kids had been there earlier in the evening and yet somehow the place was spotless. At a quick glance, everything looked perfect, and Hamilton's mom, who looked more exhausted than me, wasn't giving things more than a quick once-over.

The whole time Hamilton and I were together, Mrs. Best didn't like me. That's an understatement. The woman hated my guts. I'd never done anything to earn her loathing. Hamilton insisted that it was just because she was overprotective, a sort of no-man-is-good-enough-for-my-daughter stance. Still, I couldn't help but take her attitude toward me personally. I'd always suspected that if I was a cooler guy—a football-quarterback, student-council-president sort of guy—Mrs. Best wouldn't have had such a problem with me spending time with her daughter.

"Don't worry, I was just leaving," I said.

"Janey, we've spoken about him being here," Mrs. Best said.

I hated being spoken about as if I weren't in the room, and at another time I might have felt compelled to comment, but something else had caught my attention.

"Janey?" I repeated.

"Mom," Hamilton said, with a fake exasperated sigh. "She calls me that sometimes," she said to me. "I hate it. It's sort of like my real name."

"Sort of," her mother said, with a shake of her head. "You planning on spending the night?" she asked me. It was her very pleasant way of telling me to get lost, and she didn't have to tell me twice.

"Good night," I said, then added, "Janey."

"Do *not* call me that," Hamilton said.

I left that night with an uneasy feeling. I couldn't get the name "Janey" out of my head. I was wondering just who she was, and if I would ever meet her.

15

I look up that Bernedorn place on the Internet. It's a state psychiatric hospital that treats patients with "serious and persistent mental illnesses." As if that isn't scary enough, I find a picture of the place that looks like it would make a good setting for a horror film. I don't want to think about Hamilton being in a place like that. I tell myself she can't really be there, that the doctors, somebody, came to their senses and realized she didn't belong in a place like that, that she really wasn't that messed up. Maybe they sent her home. Maybe they were treating her as an outpatient.

I start calling her cell phone. At first I just wait and see if anyone will pick up, and when no one does, I hang up. Then, after the fourth or fifth day of this, I decide to leave a message. I'm not sure who I am leaving it for.

"Hi. This is Alex," I say. "I want to talk to you. I'm sorry. Call me back."

I don't know how many times I leave some variation of this message, but one day, when I'm getting ready to leave another message, someone answers.

"Hamilton?" I say, hopeful.

"Why couldn't you just leave her alone?" The dry voice belongs to Hamilton's mother.

"This isn't my fault," I say defensively.

"She was fine until she met you."

"That's not true," I say. "You didn't really know her."

"You think I don't know my own daughter? You think I'm stupid? You don't know what you're talking about. You're nothing but a punk."

She hangs up on me, and I realize I wasted my opportunity. I don't even know if Hamilton is still at that Bernedorn place or how she's doing. Instead of criticizing Mrs. Best's lack of parenting skills, I should try to find out how Hamilton is. I consider calling back, but figure I will just get voicemail.

Why did I have to say that? The woman makes me so mad—if she'd just paid a little more attention to her daughter, it wouldn't have fallen to me to try and make things right. If she'd just paid a little more attention from the beginning, none of this would have ever happened.

And while I might have missed out on knowing Hamilton and the clique, maybe I would have gotten the chance to know Janey. Maybe she would have turned out to be a girl who was in the color guard, collected Pez dispensers, and wanted to be a veterinarian. Maybe I would grow bored of her, but maybe she would have been the sort of person who never stopped being interesting to me.

16

Zelda was the one who told me about Janey, about why Hamilton became Hamilton. Of all the members of the clique, I spent the least time with Zelda, but that's not because I didn't like her. It was just that Zelda was more aloof. Perhaps the least likely member of the clique, she was also the most reluctant.

The summer before senior year, I had a job working at the food court at the mall. It was horrible. The only good thing about it was that sometimes Hamilton or one of the girls would stop by to visit and we would hang out for a few minutes on my break. Still, I was surprised when Zelda showed up one afternoon.

"This doesn't seem like your scene," I said.

"What? Freak girls aren't supposed to go back-to-school shopping?"

She had only a small bag in her hand.

"Doesn't look like you found much," I said.

She reached into the bag and pulled out her purchase, a single black T-shirt.

"I'm not an early riser," she said. "I don't usually have much say in the day's outfit."

The admission surprised me. Though the girls in the clique regularly made reference to each other, it was always as if they were actual separate individuals, not as if they were personalities that shared the same body. I'd been pretty sure they weren't aware of their unusual situation.

"Do you have time to talk?" Zelda asked.

I told my boss I was going to take my break and he began to expound on the sweet innocence of young love. If Zelda hadn't been there he would have told me that my girlfriend had me completely wrapped around her finger and if I didn't watch out I would be walking down the aisle before I was old enough to partake in the champagne toast. He was full of sage advice.

Zelda didn't want to sit at one of the food court tables. She insisted on standing outside, in the smoking area, even though neither one of us smoked, even though it was about 95 degrees outside.

"Things aren't going well for Hamilton," Zelda said as we sat sweating beneath the fierce summer sun. "I thought you should know, and she's not going to tell you."

"What do you mean?"

"This is going to be a rough year for her."

I thought of what Hamilton had said about graduation, that night after her party.

"Is there something I can do?"

"Just be there for her. Don't let her down."

It was a request I should have been able to comply with. I blotted my damp forehead with the back of my hand.

"You know," Zelda said, "before high school, there was no clique. It was just Hamilton and Olivia."

"For how long?" I asked.

"What do you mean?"

"For how long was Olivia part of things?"

"Forever," Zelda said. Then, in a quieter voice, she added, "Almost forever."

"What about Janey?" I asked. That was the other thing that I hadn't quite managed to put out of my mind.

Zelda's expression darkened. I knew I was treading on dangerous ground, but I couldn't help myself.

"Not quite as long as that," Zelda said quietly.

"Maybe you should start at the beginning," I suggested.

"The beginning," she repeated, trying the idea on for size. She shook her head. If I didn't go back inside soon, there would be a lecture from my boss. I was thinking maybe I should get back to work, back to what would likely be a more pleasant environment, when Zelda said, "She was a scared little girl. She never did anything to deserve what happened to her."

I knew she meant Janey. Her voice was soft. Her eyes looked sad and haunted. She looked so unlike Hamilton, I almost could believe she was a completely separate person.

"Janey never knew her real dad," Zelda continued. "Her mom had a fling with some guy who left town long before Janey was ever born, or he was married to another woman, or her conception was the result of some barely remembered one night stand. The details are a bit muddy. She was a toddler when her mother met Tom. She was three and a half when she was the flower girl at their wedding. Her mother thought it would be good for Janey to have a man around, a father figure. Tom wasn't the right man for the job."

"He hurt her," I said. I am not one of those violent, testosterone-laden sort of guys with a penchant for contact sports, but at that moment, had Tom been anywhere in the vicinity, I could have done that man serious harm. I could have killed him.

"Yes," Zelda said. Her voice was nothing but a whisper. "Tom had something wrong with him. Seriously wrong with him. The man was a complete monster."

"Did it happen more than once?"

Zelda nodded.

"He was alone with her at night, when her mom was at work."

"Where is he?" I asked. I don't know what I was thinking—that I would hunt him down and make him pay? I was not being at all rational.

"Her mom made him go away when she found out."

"How old was Hamilton then?"

"Five. It's not something five-year-olds are equipped to deal with."

I reached for her. I wanted to hold her and comfort her. I wanted to stroke her hair and tell her that I would never let anyone hurt her again. She shied away from me. I had forgotten she was Zelda, not Hamilton.

I understood how it must have been. Janey scared, unable to deal with what had happened to her, developed another persona who was everything that she was not: smart, strong, powerful, and fearless. She let her take over.

But surely someone must have realized what was going on. She would have received medical treatment. There would have been a therapist of some sort, someone to help her work through her trauma. Why wouldn't they have recognized what was going on? But I knew the answer.

"Did she see anyone?" I asked. "A child psychologist? A doctor?"

"There was a therapist she saw for a little while, but then she started school and she seemed to be doing really well, and it was like she was okay."

"But she wasn't okay."

"Her mom just wanted Janey to have a normal childhood."

"Normal?" There had been nothing normal about Hamilton's childhood. She was light years away from normal. "Maybe her mom just didn't want to face up to the fact that she was the one who'd married that creep. Maybe that's why her daughter stopped seeing the therapist." I was so angry that the words flew off my lips in an angry snarl.

"Why dredge up bad memories? What good would that have done?"

"That's not how it works," I said. "You can't just expect something like that to go away." I thought about that little girl, Janey. Was she still in there somewhere? "What happened to Janey?" I asked.

"Her mom let her pick a new name."

"Pick a new name?"

"So she could have a fresh start," Zelda explained.

"Or so her mom wouldn't be held liable for what she let happen to her daughter." I couldn't believe it. It's like Hamilton's mom had gone out of her way to do everything she wasn't supposed to do.

"She made him go away," Zelda said.

"Too little, too late."

If I didn't go back inside soon, I wouldn't have a job anymore. But I didn't care.

"So where did Hamilton come from?" I asked.

"Come from?"

"Her name—the name Hamilton—where did it come from?"

"I'm not sure. I think there was a stuffed animal or something."

"Jesus." I swiped my arm across my damp forehead. "Don't you think that's kind of messed up?" Then I remembered who I was talking to. I was talking to one of my girlfriend's alternate personalities. A girl named Zelda, who I doubted anyone besides me and my girlfriend and her other personalities even knew about. Really, it made no sense to ask about things being messed up.

"They did okay on their own for a while," Zelda said.

"Janey and her mom?"

"Hamilton and Olivia."

To me, Zelda's definition of okay and the rest of the world's definition of okay seemed like two very different things.

"Adolescence hasn't been easy," Zelda added. "That's why she started the clique, and we've been there to help her and all. But you can't stay a kid forever. When you become an adult, people expect you to stand on your own. Hamilton doesn't know how to be alone."

"She doesn't have to be," I said. I reached for her again, momentarily forgetting who she was, and she gave me a cold, icy stare.

"Maybe we're all ready to grow up," she said. She stared off into space, with that hard Zelda set to her jaw.

17

Finding Bernedorn Psychiatric Hospital is easy. Getting in to see Hamilton is another matter. The desk clerk wants me to produce a family tree to prove I'm a blood relative.

"It's very important that I see her," I say.

"She's ill. She's been undergoing treatment."

"What are you doing to her?" My voice comes out in an angry shout. In my head I picture shock treatment, ugly horror-movie-inspired devices.

"If you're going to take that tone with me, then I'm going to have to ask you to leave."

I note that she did not answer my question, but I comply and walk away.

Prom is this weekend. A few months ago, I couldn't have imagined not going with Hamilton, but now it's a relief not to be going, a relief not to have to face the stares, to try and ignore their whispers every time they think I'm not paying attention. If things hadn't changed, if everything had stayed how it was, then I would have taken Hamilton to the prom. Of course, that would have proved to be something of a nightmare as well. An event like that ... all of them would have wanted to be part of the action. I would have been something of a babysitter, corralling her, keeping her from doing or saying the wrong thing to one of our fellow students, keeping her from being torn to pieces there on the dance floor. It makes me wonder if all the work I did—running after her, keeping things in line, all the parties—was only prolonging the inevitable. Hamilton was nothing but a time bomb. Perhaps the question had never been if she was going to self-destruct, but when.

I keep telling myself it's a good thing I'm not going to the prom with Hamilton. But despite trying to visualize the chaos, the nightmare it would have been, I mostly imagine her sparkling and shining and utterly and completely happy.

The morning of the prom, I wake up with an empty feeling. I've missed Hamilton for so long, and I know this day shouldn't be any different, but it is. The ache and the longing is too powerful to ignore. I have to see her.

I don't know how I am going to get into Bernedorn. I only know I'm an idiot for letting that clerk push me around last time. Hamilton wouldn't have taken no for an answer.

On the way to the psychiatric hospital, I formulate a

plan. When I walk into the reception area, I'll be a different person. They will let me in. My confident swagger will be more than just an act.

It's a different clerk at the desk; already it's like things are going my way. This clerk has her face buried in a paperback book. She looks up only long enough to size me up.

"Hey," I say, like I do this all the time, "I'm here to see Janey Best. I'm her physics lab partner." The words are unpremeditated, but it sure sounds like I know what I'm talking about.

"Relatives only," she says. The book must be a good one, because she's returned her attention to its pages.

"Yeah, look, where's the clerk who's here normally? During the week?"

"She's got the day off," this clerk says, her eyes still glued to the book.

"Right, 'cause I'd worked everything out with her. I had a note from school."

The woman holds out her hand for the note, still without looking up. Crap, why did I have to say that about the note?

"Well, I gave it to the other clerk. The one who's here normally. I think she made a note of it or something."

"Computers are down," the clerk says.

"Right. Well, it's kind of important that I see Janey today. We have this big project due Monday."

She finally puts down the book and gives me a pretty thorough looking-over. Apparently I pass muster, because she begins filling out a visitor's pass with a black magic marker.

"I need to see your ID," she says. I calmly hand it over while inside my head, my brain has taken up a silent *Yes! Yes! Yes!* cheer.

After I get myself all logged in, the clerk sends me on the way with a pass, eagerly returning to her book. I almost slip up and ask her how to find Hamilton's room, then realize I can't ask something so completely stupid.

So instead, I set out in what looks to be the right direction. I study my visitor's pass, which has some cryptic information on it. Perhaps it directs me to where I can find Hamilton, but I can't make sense of it.

I spy an elevator. Getting on seems like a wise idea, but when I do, I realize I have to pick a floor. There are three more of them besides this one, not to mention a basement. I'm picturing a basement filled with old medical records and the pervasive smell of damp. On a whim, I hit the button labeled B.

The basement isn't as bad as I'd pictured it. I see what I'm looking for, and wandering in what I hope looks to be a lost and confused fashion, I go past the door to the janitor's office.

"Can I help you?" says the old, scruffy man inside. He doesn't get up from the table he's sitting at. I feign surprise at his question.

"I think I must have gotten off at the wrong floor," I say. "I'm here to visit a friend of mine, a classmate."

"You want two," he says. "That's where they have all the kids."

"Right," I say. "Thanks."

When I get off the elevator on the second floor, there are two ways I can go. To the right is a mural featuring all sorts of brightly colored zoo animals. Do they think teenagers would be comforted by the childish images? Then I get to thinking about those brightly colored animals. Are there actually little kids in this place? There must be, if they have something like that. I feel bad for these kids, and briefly toy with the idea of running in and releasing them like some sort of deranged superhero. No, then they would probably kick me out before I had a chance to see Hamilton. Either that or they would lock me up in this place, convinced of my own insanity.

Besides, maybe it's better for those kids to get fixed young. Hamilton probably wouldn't be here now if she'd gotten treatment as a child. In fact, Hamilton probably wouldn't be in the world at all if Janey had gone to a place like this as a kid. She'd just be some random, ordinary teenager living some normal life. It makes me sad and scared at the same time.

Heading in the opposite direction of the animal mural, I find myself walking down a corridor that has the look of someone trying a bit too hard to cater to teenagers. There are plenty of dark colors here, with a bright accent or two. When I come to a set of double doors done in a horrible paint-splatter effect, any doubts about where to go are instantly erased. I've most certainly found the teen wing.

Janey is in the common room, I'm told. One of the staff members leads me back there. We pass by a series of tiny bedrooms—in some of them I see kids sitting on beds. There are other teens roaming the hall. Everyone looks drugged and dazed. Is this what crazy looks like? I realize that they probably are drugged. It makes me scared to see what Hamilton will look like.

The common room is as depressing as the rest of the place. One wall is all windows, but they don't open. They look out onto a field of dead brown grass. There's a tiny television that a bunch of kids are gathered around. Some ancient-looking computers hum away in one corner, and there's a sad little bookshelf full of faded paperbacks. I look around, and at first I don't see her. Then the girl curled up in one of the chairs moves, and I recognize her.

Her hair looks greasy and unwashed. She's dressed in a faded T-shirt and sweats. Her color is all wrong. Her skin looks almost gray beneath the room's fluorescent lighting. The shock of seeing her like that makes me flinch.

"Hamilton?" I ask. It's nothing but a guess. I can't tell who she is.

"Alex," she says. Her voice is so flat and emotionless, that she sounds a million miles away.

"How are you?" I ask.

She shrugs. She looks out the windows with their depressing view.

"This place," I say, but don't know how to finish the sentence. I was going to say something like *This place is a nightmare*, but I realize that sounds a bit tactless, especially since it's a nightmare she's trapped in.

"It's hell," she says, in that same unfamiliar, flat voice. Is she Hamilton? I can't even tell. "I didn't expect you to come here."

"I've missed you," I say. "A lot."

"I miss everyone," she says, and I hear just a trace of emotion in her voice, a hint of sadness.

"School's not the same without you," I say.

"I can't imagine what they're saying," she says. She's still looking out the window. I can't tell if she's crying, but it almost sounds like she might be. In a quieter voice she says, "I hardly know who I am anymore."

Music begins to play. Strange, almost haphazard digital notes fill the air. I turn around and see a tired old digital keyboard and a girl with that same dazed, washed-out look that Hamilton has, hitting the keys.

"You're you," I say. Hamilton turns and looks at me.

"Whoever the hell that is," she says ruefully.

"It's for the best, all this," I say. I don't know if I'm trying to convince her or reassure myself. "You should have gotten this help a long time ago. It's your mother's fault. She screwed up big time."

"No. She did what had to be done." She looks away from me again.

I think she's pissed at me. Damn it. Why did I have to say that about her mother? It's true, but I should have just kept my mouth shut.

"She worked hard to keep a roof over our heads, to buy me clothes. She did everything for me," Hamilton says.

"If she really cared about you, she would have tried to find someone to help you." As I say the words, I realize I'm implicating myself. By my own reasoning, if I really cared about Hamilton, then I should have helped her instead of being her enabler.

"She was so busy with work, so tired. She never really knew. She thought Olivia was some friend of mine from school because that's what I told her. Because that's what I believed."

I find it hard to believe her mother didn't know something was seriously wrong, but she spent a lot of time working and slept when she was home during the day. Perhaps Mrs. Best had been as fooled as everyone else. In which case, I really am the bad guy. I alone knew Hamilton's secret.

"Hamilton?" I say. I want to reach out and touch her, to push her unwashed hair out of her face, but something stops me. It feels like it would be out of line, somehow. Not because I'd be violating some sort of visitor-patient conduct policy, but because I'm not quite sure who Hamilton is. There's something off about her, something not right.

"Look, the thing is, you should really call me Janey."

"Janey," I repeat. I recall that time, nearly a year ago now, when she told me to never call her that. "Is that who you are?"

"It's who I am," Hamilton says. "It's who I've always

been." Her hollow, empty voice doesn't sound so sure. I don't want to call her Janey—I don't know who Janey is.

"What about Hamilton?" I ask.

"I've been working with a psychiatrist," she says. "She wants me to use my real name, to try and just be me, you know."

"So, what? Everyone starts calling you Janey and that's it? You're suddenly cured?" I hear the anger in my voice, and I hate myself for being like this, but I can't help it. I don't want Janey. I want my girlfriend back. I want Hamilton and the rest of them.

Hamilton, Janey, whoever the hell she is, walks over to the windows and looks out at the withered landscape. Is this slouched girl in her ragged clothes Janey? Who is Janey to me?

"Hey," I say. "You know, we're missing the prom this weekend."

That gets her to turn around and look at me. She gives me a crooked smile and almost looks like her old self. "I didn't really think that was your sort of thing, Alex."

"I would have to be an idiot to pass up an opportunity to dance with the most beautiful girl in Fidelity. What do you say?" I hold out my hand to her.

She just stares at me like I'm crazy. "I'm not dressed for it, and something tells me I'm not going to get a day pass to attend the prom."

"Can I have one dance, at least?"

"Here? There isn't even any music."

I turn to the girl at the keyboard.

"Can you play us a love song?" I ask. The girl looks up at me, then returns to her same discordant melody. It'll have to do.

Hamilton takes my hand. She's still looking at me like I'm the crazy one, and she might be more than a little bit right. I take her in my arms and dance with her in that sad, shabby room. I close my eyes; I can see her in her gown, can feel the stares of our classmates, not the stares of the other patients, as we glide across the dance floor.

18

When senior year started, things were different. Worse. Suddenly every day was like a party, and I don't mean that in a good way. Keeping track of who Hamilton was from one class period to the next was almost impossible. I couldn't be by her side all day long, which meant I couldn't protect her. I had to just trust in the fact that she had the strength to hold it all together, although that was looking less and less likely with each passing day. I was scared, and so was she.

"I wish life had a pause button," Hamilton said to me one afternoon as we sat on her front steps. The sun was low in the sky and the last rays of autumn sunshine were not quite enough to keep the chill out of the air. I put my arm around her and she rested her head on my shoulder. "Better yet, a rewind button."

"How far back would you want to go?" I asked. I was

hurt by her remark. I didn't want to be anywhere else but right where I was.

"Last year. The year before that. I don't know. Fourth grade was nice, or maybe third."

I hadn't known Hamilton in third or fourth grade. I didn't want to go back that far.

"What's wrong with right now?" I asked.

"Things are moving too fast. Before you know it, we'll be graduating, and it's like everything will be over before it even started."

"There is life after graduation," I said, again.

"Maybe," she said, as if it were open for debate. I realize now that she already knew the natives were getting restless. She could feel them straining and pulling in their own separate directions. I'd noticed the change in her, but I hadn't understood what it meant.

"Speaking of going back in time," I said, "I was trying to track down some information about your stepfather."

"What?" Hamilton pulled away and stared at me in alarm. "Why would you do something like that?"

I don't know why I'd expected her to be on board with that. I knew it was a sensitive area, but I thought maybe it was what she needed to help heal. It's what I would have wanted, if I were her. But then, it wasn't like Hamilton had ever talked about it with me. I think she knew I knew, but it wasn't a subject she'd ever brought up. Zelda was the one who'd told me. Hamilton had never breathed a word.

Still, I thought it would help her if she could just see things the way I saw them.

"Look, after what he did, he deserves to be punished, locked up."

"Just forget it," Hamilton said. "It was a long time ago."

"I can't rest easy knowing he's out there," I said. "What if he tries to hurt another little girl?"

"I'm sure that's not going to happen."

"But you don't know that."

"Just drop it, Alex."

She shifted away from me, and without her warmth beside me, I felt the chill of the air cut through my clothes. Hamilton may have convinced herself that it was all behind her, but obviously she was wrong. I wasn't content to let that man escape justice. One way or another, he would pay for what he did.

19

A light drizzle falls on me as I slip out the back doors instead of eating whatever unappetizing dish the cafeteria has on the menu. I want to be alone. I can't stand listening to any more stupid high school chatter. Things have reached a fever pitch. It must be like this every year as the end of school approaches, but I never really noticed before.

The week after prom, I returned to school feeling worse than ever. Visiting Hamilton didn't erase my longing and loneliness. If anything, I missed her more than ever. That girl in the hospital, Janey or whoever she was, was just a shadow of the girl I used to know. I didn't see how being in that place was helping her at all. Maybe that's why her mother ignored what should have been obvious warning signs—maybe that's why, way back, she discontinued Janey's therapy after only a few sessions. She might have realized that her daughter's way of dealing with things was better than anything the medical profession could do for her. I knew I was grasping at straws, but I felt a bit vindicated. Maybe I wasn't such a bad guy for keeping Hamilton's secret. Better that than turning her into this vague shadow of a girl, I told myself.

As if in solidarity with the girl I loved, I drifted through the next several weeks in a daze as deep as any drugged-out psychiatric hospital patient. I went through the motions of being a high school senior without actually really experiencing anything. The only time I felt any emotion was when I worried that graduation was arriving too quickly (Hamilton had pegged that one). I desperately wanted things to slow down. It was bad enough she'd missed the prom, but Hamilton was going to freak if she missed graduation. That is, if she still had the mental ability to freak out. I wasn't sure, after seeing her looking so wasted.

"It's just going to feel so weird."

The girl's voice startles me. I slide back against the building, press myself against the wall. Apparently I'm not alone out here.

"Well, I heard maybe Chrissy is going to throw a party," another girl says.

"Like that would even be anything close," the first girl says. "You know, I already knew what I was going to wear and everything."

"Well, that's jumping the gun. How do you even know you would have made the guest list?"

"I don't know. Maybe she'll be back before graduation."

"I wouldn't count on it. I heard she had, like, a lobotomy or something."

Is that the rumor going around now? Unbelievable. I resist the urge to correct them and instead slip around the other side of the building. Since Hamilton's been gone, I've heard all sorts of explanations of what's happened to her, some far-fetched and some a little too close to the truth. The most common explanation is that she had a nervous breakdown. Most kids seem to assume that the pressures of being the most popular girl in school finally became too much for her. While I haven't been actively spreading this rumor, I've also never attempted to dispel it. It's close enough to the truth without making her look like a complete and total freak. So I'm okay with it.

And these girls aren't the only ones who miss Hamilton's parties—they were a nightmare for me, sure, but just being able to see Hamilton in her element, looking so happy, basking in the adoration of her classmates, was worth all the running around, all the shepherding I had to do.

An all-too-familiar battered green station wagon is parked in one of the visitor spaces, and I stop short. What is Mrs. Best's car doing here? Panic and hope simultaneously seize hold of me, and I start jogging toward the car.

It's empty, but as I come around it I see Hamilton standing there, leaning against the door. She's a shadow of the girl I used to know, but she looks better than when I saw her in the hospital.

"Are you . . . ?" I don't know how to finish the question. I'm not sure what I am asking.

"Free as a bird?" she asks. There's something about the dry tone of her voice that catches me off-guard.

"Olivia?"

"I'm just Janey, Alex," she says. Even though I know this is a good thing, my heart sinks a little bit.

"So, when are you coming back to school?"

"I'm still on house arrest for a while. I'm still in treatment. It's probably best that I don't return, you know."

"No, I don't know."

"Look at me, Alex. I don't belong here. I can see that. They all think I'm a complete headcase. And they're right."

I think of the two girls I overhead talking about the alleged lobotomy, but I also remember what started that conversation. They were talking about missing Hamilton's end-of-the-year party.

Hamilton—Janey—whoever the hell she is—refuses to look at me. She stares down at her shoes as if she was Nordica. When I reach to brush her hair from her face, she shies away from me and blushes. She's acting just like Nordica right now.

"Hamilton?" I say, just to be sure.

"Janey," she says. Crap, right. It's going to take me some time to get used to that name.

"I love you," I say.

"Well, at least somebody does."

"You have no idea," I say.

I look up and see Hamilton's mom coming down the

sidewalk. I don't really want to be around when she gets here. "I should probably get back to class."

I walk away from her, feeling even worse than before. I look back at her standing there, looking so sad and alone, and I resolve to make it up to her.

20

Things kept getting worse. Our first year together, Hamilton's personality changes weren't that frequent. It used to be that when she was Hamilton, or whoever, she'd stay whoever she happened to be for at least a little while. I knew there was internal strife; I heard about disagreements between different members of the clique, but I never saw those disagreements. That all changed senior year.

As graduation inched closer, the internal strife kicked up a notch and suddenly wasn't so internal. I found myself in the bewildering position of talking to more than one member of the clique at a time. It was confusing and unnerving, but at least I could grasp what was going on. What would happen, I wondered, if her warring personalities were to put in an appearance when she was talking to someone who didn't know what was going on. It would be a complete disaster. Still, what really scared me was the way Hamilton seemed to be losing control.

The thing is, she'd never *seemed* crazy before. She'd seemed mildly eccentric at worst, but this heightened intensity made me see everything in a new light. She was more and more scattered, like she couldn't even keep track of who she was anymore. I knew now that Hamilton needed serious help.

Right before her Christmas party, I saw her in the hallway after school. She was Shelly, but she was also Olivia. They were having some sort of disagreement about decorations for the party.

"No, we can't just 'toss some tinsel around,'" Shelly was saying. "I printed up a list of the decorating supplies we'll need. Did you even look at it?"

"My mistake," Olivia said. "I thought that was an inventory of all the holiday decorations at the party store."

"Apparently, I have to do everything myself around here. Forget it. I'll go pick up the decorations. You just need to burn the Christmas mix CDs."

"No."

"Excuse me?"

"God, Shelly, can't you do that in the bathroom? That's why I brown-bag it on taco day."

"Listen, you obnoxious bitch, I'm just asking you to do one little favor for me."

"Well, when you put it that way, no."

She spun around and saw me standing there. I'm sure

my face registered shock, possibly alarm. My mouth may have been hanging open.

"Alex," she said, in a falsely sweet Shelly voice.

"Is everything all right?" I asked.

"Oh, just ducky. Olivia and I were just going over plans for the Holiday Bash."

"Of course," I said. "I'll catch you later." I took off down the hallway. She called something after me, something about the party, but I didn't stop to listen. Watching her arguing with herself had been frightening. I was covered in a thin layer of sweat, and I wasn't sure where I was running to until I burst through the door of the guidance office.

"Can I help you?" the secretary at the desk asked.

"Is the school psychologist here?" I asked.

"Oh. She left a short while ago." The secretary looked at my sweaty face and the wild look in my eyes and concluded I was in desperate need of professional help. "Let me get you the emergency number."

I left with the number, but I never called. I came to my senses. I realized, again, that I couldn't do that to Hamilton, no matter how crazy things had gotten. To turn her in like that would have been heartless even if I was doing it for her own good.

I called another number instead, my hand shaking as I dialed. When she answered, I was too scared to speak.

"Hello?" she said for the third time, in an annoyed tone. I sensed she was about to hang up.

"Wait," I said. "It's Alex."

"What do you want?" Mrs. Best said. "She's not home yet."

"I know. I want to talk to you about her. There's something you ought to know." My heart raced. I wasn't sure I really wanted to do this, but then I recalled the argument I'd witnessed. I tried to tell myself it was a one-time thing, but I knew that wasn't true. There'd been other warning signs.

"Hah. You think there's something you can tell me about my own daughter? I know her better than you ever will," Mrs. Best said.

"I'm not sure that you do," I said.

"Oh, believe me, bub, I do. So I think maybe you need to find someone else to bug."

"But—"

"Leave her alone, do you hear me?"

She hung up on me. There was no reasoning with the woman.

Maybe it was for the best. She'd had years to help her daughter and didn't do a thing; she even took Hamilton out of therapy. She let her five-year-old pick out a new name for herself. She assumed Olivia was simply some friend from school even though she'd never met her. For years, the woman saw whatever it was that she wanted to see. Maybe she really didn't know, maybe she did. Either way, Hamilton could have benefited from a bit more of her attention.

I wondered if the reason she hated me was not because she didn't think I was good enough for her daughter, but because I actually knew Hamilton better than she did.

21

The lady in the office starts writing out a late pass as soon as I walk in.

"No, I don't need a late pass," I explain. "I'm in study hall right now." She looks at me skeptically, as if I might be confused about things. "I came down here to get a list of all the students in the school."

She laughs like I've just told a hilarious joke.

"What are you really doing here?" she asks, when her giggles have subsided.

"Please," I explain. "It's no big deal. I'm sure you could just press a button and get the whole thing run off."

"I can't just print you out a list of all the students in the school."

"I don't want their phone numbers or their GPAs or anything, just their names. That's public information."

"It's not something we do," she says. I can tell she's not

going to budge on this. "Why don't you just look in your yearbook? All the names will be in there."

My apathy about the high school social scene has come back to bite me in the butt. I don't actually have a yearbook, have never signed up to get one. I didn't see the point of it. I suppose Hamilton ordered one, but that doesn't help me now. I'm going to have to find someone willing to lend me a yearbook.

I don't know where Jasmine's locker is, but it doesn't take me long to find it. I scan the lunchtime locker crowd. I look for someone dressed like an oddball and spy a pair of zebra-striped tights with a skirt that even fashion-challenged me can see clashes horribly.

"I need to borrow your yearbook," I say.

"Alex, hey," she says. "Did you want to come have lunch with me?"

"I don't have time," I say. "I kind of need to use your yearbook for something."

"I don't have a yearbook," she says. She gives a sheepish shrug. "I don't really know anyone, you know, so I didn't see the point in getting a yearbook. I'm not very good at making friends, I guess."

"Don't you know anyone you could borrow a yearbook from?"

"What about you? You're, like, the most popular guy in the school."

I laugh at her. "Me? I'm a complete loser."

"I'll see what I can do," she says with a sigh.

Even in a tiny font, the list takes up twelve pages. The bulletin board is only so big. I paper over it, and even then some of the pages spill over onto the wall around it. It's a sloppy mess, but it's an eye-catching sloppy mess. I smile to myself.

The next morning the crowd clogs the hallway. I've never seen this many people crowded around one of Hamilton's lists before, but then, Hamilton's lists never took quite so long to read. It's silly, I know. I could have just posted a notice that everyone was invited, saving myself the trouble of typing up this list and saving everyone else the trouble of reading it, but there's no fun in that. Besides, that misses the point. The point is to be singled out, to be special, to feel that joy that comes from seeing your own name up there on one of Hamilton's infamous guest lists.

There are some whispers and murmurings. Some people are not sure the list is for real. How could Hamilton throw a party if she's locked up in a loony bin somewhere? Since when has Hamilton invited so many people to a party before? The dissenting voices, though, are in the minority. Most of the assembled students gladly accept the posted list as gospel. They want to believe.

Most of them study the list looking for their name and the names of their friends; perhaps, after the rumor spreads through the school that everybody is on the list, they won't be studying it so hard. Either way, I figure that no one is going to notice four extra names on this list, four names that have never been there before. Perhaps someone will wonder as they stumble over one of the unfamiliar names, but then assume it's just some student they don't know.

It was something I needed to do.

It was wishful thinking on my part, of course. Maybe it was something else as well—justice. They'd done their time here just like anyone else, but their names would never appear in any yearbook. They would be left off the commencement roll. I didn't want them to be wiped away as if they'd never existed.

I didn't count on Jasmine. She finds me at my locker. She's holding the yearbook that she'd borrowed from the girl in her math class for me.

"I went through this three times," Jasmine says.

"It's not like there's going to be a quiz," I say.

"There's no one named Zelda in here, or Olivia or Nordica."

"You left out Shelly. Did you check every name on the list against the book? That must have taken a long time."

"Just the weird ones. Zelda is the name she used that day she had on the purple dress. She told me her name was Zelda."

"Who knew it was such a common name?" I shut my locker and start to head down the hall.

Jasmine doesn't take the hint. She follows at my heels.

"It's not a common name. Who is this Zelda? And Olivia and Nordica, and the other one you mentioned, Shelly?"

"Inside joke," I tell her. "I find it interesting that you're paying so much attention to the guest list. You never did before."

"Who are they?"

"By the way, did you notice that your name's on there?"

"You're not going to answer me, are you?"

I'm beginning to regret putting Jasmine on the list. It would have been pretty mean to exclude her, especially after she borrowed that yearbook for me, but she can be really annoying.

"Why do you care so much?" I ask.

"It's why she sometimes sat alone at lunch, isn't it?"

I realize I might have gone too far. I hadn't really counted on Jasmine conducting her own research project. The girl's too nosy and too smart. I'm afraid to say anything, sure that I will accidentally spill the secret I've helped to keep hidden for so long.

"I've got to go," I tell her. "I've got something I need to do."

22

Probably one of the most difficult things about dating Hamilton was how I had to adjust my own behavior to match whoever she was at the moment. If she was Hamilton, I was her boyfriend, but if she was one of the other girls, then I was only her friend's boyfriend. Big difference. I forgot a lot, and other times maybe I didn't forget so much as ignore the fact that she was someone else.

I mean, sure, it's wrong to kiss your girlfriend's best friend, but what if the best friend is just another personality that lives in your girlfriend's body? I mean, if she's still deep down your girlfriend, it shouldn't matter, right?

And the thing was, I loved her. All of her, not just the Hamilton part of her. Even Shelly had her appeal. It would be like if you were dating someone and they had some sort of secret life that you didn't know about at first. Like maybe they had their own late-night talk radio show or some secret blog and then you found out about it, and you liked the way they were sort of like this different person when they were on the radio or writing their blog or whatever. I mean, that's still part of who they are, and you wouldn't be wrong for falling in love with them all over again when you heard their voice on the radio or read the things they had written. It was sort of like that, but a tiny bit different.

My guess is, if you told your girlfriend that you'd heard her secret radio show and fallen in love with her all over again, she wouldn't act like you were saying something completely outrageous, or like you were betraying her in any way. Yet it didn't work that way with Hamilton. It wasn't like I was in love with five different girls. I was in love with just one girl. At least, that's what I told myself.

But then, when she was Olivia and told me she didn't love me, or that she liked Chance Avanale, it was like a punch in the gut. She wasn't doing it to be mean. She couldn't know how it would hurt me. Still, I didn't know how she couldn't understand. It didn't seem possible that she could be so blind.

It became even more confusing for me as she got worse. I found her, one evening, posting the guest list. Hamilton always posted the lists, but she wasn't acting like herself. I watched her as she tried to staple the list to the bulletin board with shaking hands. It took her several tries, and at one point she gave herself a paper cut.

"Hamilton?" I asked.

"Oh!" she cried out. She was so startled, she dropped

the stapler. It fell with a loud crash on the floor, echoing down the empty hallway. She blushed, and her eyes were big and scared like a deer caught in the headlights. "Alex," she said. "What are you doing here?"

"Detention," I said. She sounded like Nordica. I was sure it was Nordica, but what was she doing putting the guest list up? Things had gotten so strange lately, I wasn't sure what was going on. "Nordica?"

"It's not what it looks like," she said. "I was just looking at the list, but it started to fall down and I was just stapling it back up."

"Oh," I said. It was a lie. I had seen her putting the list up. I didn't say anything, though. She wouldn't meet my eye. I wanted to wrap my arms around her and hold her tight, tell her everything would be fine and that she didn't have to worry.

I reached for her but she backed up, muttered something about having to leave, and ran down the hallway. I wondered if it had gotten so bad she was getting confused, forgetting who she was and what she was supposed to do. Instead of leaving, I roamed the school thinking about her, about how strange things had become. Maybe I could lie and tell myself she had it all together before, but now, she was looking more and more like someone who didn't have it together at all. Could I just stand there and let her fall apart?

It wasn't much later that she came back. She was in the same spot she was in before, in front of the bulletin board. She looked as confused as I felt. I was sure she must be

Hamilton this time, but I was wrong. She was Olivia. She had some excuse about looking for her physics book. She was lying to me, just like she'd done when she was Nordica, but Olivia didn't shy away from me. She let me kiss her. Even though I knew it proved she was more confused than ever, I didn't care because I thought maybe somehow I could help her keep it all together. The two of us (or the six of us) could figure out some way to make it all work, to keep her on track. It beat the alternative.

23

Graduation is just around the corner and I've turned in all my assignments, but I still have one research project to complete. It's not one I'll be graded on, but I know it's more important than any work I've ever done for school. In the end, everything can be traced back to one man. Hamilton's stepfather is the root of all evil, as far as I am concerned. He's the one who drove her off the deep end, and it's been his evil presence lurking in the shadows all these years. I know that if I can somehow track him down, it might be enough to give her the closure she needs to bounce back and get on with her life. I'll find this bastard, and one way or another find a way for Hamilton to put her demons to bed.

The only guy I've turned up looks like a dead end. He's got the right name, but other than that, there's nothing to indicate he's the man I'm looking for. What I need is someone with a clear link to Fidelity; it's the only way I'll know I've found him. I could try to do some sort of public records search to see if I can turn up a marriage certificate, something that would make it clear he lived here at some point. Instead, I sit here at one of the public library's Internet stations, playing around with desperate Google searches to no avail.

"Who's that guy?"

I spin around. Jasmine is standing right behind me.

"None of your business," I mutter. I quickly kill the screen.

"Are you trying to hunt down your birth father or something?"

"No." I wish she would leave me alone, but then I wonder. Jasmine's smart and persistent, and just maybe she would know how to find someone. "Okay, yes," I say. "I was given up for adoption when I was a baby. I'm doing some family research. I don't know much, but I know he lived in Fidelity when I was younger." I sound like I'm lying, but Jasmine seems to buy it.

"You should look in the *Fidelity News Weekly*," she says. "The old issues aren't archived online, but the library has it all on microfilm."

"Why do you know this?"

"There's not a lot to do around here for a friendless freak like me," she says with a shrug. I stare at her. It's the stupidest explanation I've ever heard. No one looks at old newspapers on microfilm just to pass the time. I keep staring at her. Eventually she caves. "I wanted to find out everything I could about Hamilton. After Google and old yearbooks, I turned to the local paper."

"And what did you find?"

"Nothing, really. She made the honor roll a bunch of times, but not much else. She apparently did a good job of staying out of the media spotlight." I snort at this.

"Well, to the microfilm it is."

Let me tell you something about microfilm. It's not a lot of fun to work with. The process is tedious. With Jasmine by my side, I scroll through page after page, issue after issue of the *Fidelity News Weekly*, not sure exactly what I'm looking for, not sure that it's even there to be found. Invariably, other headlines grab my attention, and I waste time reading some thirteen-year-old news story.

I think about Jasmine and all the time she spent going through microfilm looking for something about Hamilton. It would have taken her hours upon hours, days. Why would she have done something like that? Could she really be that obsessed with Hamilton? The answer is obviously yes, but I don't understand it.

"You really looked through all this stuff looking for something about Hamilton?" I ask.

"I didn't have anything better to do."

"You realize this makes you seem kind of creepy and obsessive."

"I don't think I'm alone in that," she says. She looks into my eyes like she knows the statement about looking for my birth father is nothing but crap. I feel myself redden, and pretend to be engrossed in some news story on the screen.

By the second paragraph, I'm no longer pretending. I glance up at the date on the top of the page. It's much later than I would have guessed, just shortly before we started high school, and the story is not at all what I'd have expected.

Oblivious, Jasmine starts to scroll forwards, but I stop her.

"Hang on," I say. "Go back."

She goes back to the page with the story. She starts reading it, then freezes when she sees the name.

"That's Hamilton's mother, isn't it?" she asks. I nod.

The summer before we started high school, apparently, the lake was dredged to make repairs on the dam. They found his body settled into the muddy lake bed. It had been there for about nine years, ever since the man had disappeared from Hamilton's life, leaving a scarred little girl in his wake. Police questioned the man's widow, and Mrs. Best alluded to her husband's drinking problem. That and the autopsy results led police to the conclusion that an excessively drunk Tom Framm had been stumbling along the bridge near the dam when he blacked out, fell into the lake, and drowned in the dark, deep water.

"Was that her father?" Jasmine asks.

"Stepfather," I say. I recall Zelda saying that Hamilton's mother had made her stepfather go away. I don't recall her mentioning a drinking problem, though.

24

Most guys are under the impression that they are way more desirable than they actually are, and Chance Avanale is one of those guys. Hamilton never paid him more than the most cursory attention, so I never worried about her breaking up with me because of him. Sure, there were things she wasn't satisfied with in our relationship, but it was sort of like in a spy movie—I knew too much. Sappy romantic that I was, though, I thought it was because she was as in love with me as I was with her.

It was Olivia, of course, who first started talking about Chance. That's when I began to have my doubts. Even though it wasn't Hamilton talking, Olivia was still Hamilton. When you hear your girlfriend singing the praises of some stupid soccer player with an annoying smirk, it doesn't really matter if it's your girlfriend or her alter ego uttering the words. You suddenly feel very vulnerable.

And then you see this same guy, all smiley, chatting with your girlfriend between classes, or him and his friends crowding around her at lunch, or the two of them almost drooling over each other at a party. So, I don't think it was all that unreasonable that I was jealous of that cocky bastard.

One day after school I happened to run into Chance in a deserted stairwell, but of course I had learned a thing or two from dating Hamilton. That chance meeting (if you'll pardon the pun) wasn't so accidental. It wasn't just luck that I was carrying a metal ruler that I'd borrowed from the mechanical drafting room. That ruler was just the right size for slipping through the handles of the doors to make sure we didn't have any company.

I feel I should point out a few things. Chance is bigger than I am. Chance plays sports—I do not. I haven't been involved in a physical fight since I was in nursery school and dumped sand on top of Timmy Rukowski's head. So, what the hell did I think I was doing, cornering Chance in a deserted stairwell? Let's just say, jealousy can make you do some peculiar shit.

"Hey," Chance said with that annoying smirk of his, like we were old buddies or something.

"Just stay the hell away from her," I said.

"Whoa, chill," Chance said. "I don't even know what you're talking about."

"Like hell you don't. Stay the hell away from my girlfriend."

"Your girlfriend?"

The questioning tone caught me off guard. Why had he phrased it like that? I knew it wasn't Hamilton who was interested in this moron, but it wasn't like anyone else knew that. It wasn't like anyone else even knew there was someone named Olivia.

Or did they? What if all this time, I'd been kidding myself that I was the only one who really knew Hamilton? What if all this time, I wasn't the only one who understood that the reason Hamilton seemed like such a well-rounded person was that she wasn't only just one person? What if Chance had figured it out? What if the whole school knew?

"Hamilton," I said, but my voice had lost its forcefulness. Even I wasn't convinced of my own words.

"I don't know what you're talking about," Chance said. "I hardly know her."

"Who *do* you know?" I said in my deflated voice. A cold hard chunk of ice seemed to have formed in my gut.

"Donna," he said. "We've been together a long time."

Donna? I fought to control my panic, to keep my cool against my romantic rival. I didn't know Donna, but was it possible there was some new personality I hadn't even met yet? Zelda had said it was Hamilton and Olivia for the longest time, but then with all the extra stress of high school, she and the others had appeared. I knew Hamilton was completely freaked out about graduation, about leaving school, so didn't it make sense she would deal with that stress the way she always had before, creating some other alter ego to help her out?

I didn't even care if there was someone new. I would

have been fine with it. What I wasn't fine with was that Chance knew this Donna personality and I'd never even met her.

"What?" Chance said. "Hey, are you all right?"

I nodded and stepped away from him. I didn't dare speak. If I did, I was afraid I'd start crying. I shuffled to the door and grabbed it, but when I pulled on it, I was met with resistance. I'd forgotten about my stupid stunt with the metal ruler, a stunt that seemed so cool and intimidating just a few minutes ago but now struck me as completely idiotic. I looked down at the stupid ruler and tears began to roll down my face.

"Hey, did she break up with you or something?" Chance asked.

"Is that what you told her to do?" I said. I didn't look at him and I tried to keep the tears out of my voice, but he could probably tell. I was pathetic.

"No. Why would I do that?"

"So you can have her all to yourself."

"Dude, I told you I'm with Donna, okay? Her mom and dad are going away this weekend and she's got the house to herself. Like I'm going to do anything to mess up that, right?"

"She doesn't have a dad," I said. "It's not like we can just share . . ."

I stopped. I remembered seeing Chance at lunch being awfully chummy with some girl in extra-tight clothes. I couldn't remember her name, but maybe it was Donna. I remember hearing some story about her getting thrown off the Students Against Drinking and Drugs committee.

"Wait. Is Donna that girl you eat lunch with, the one with the drinking problem?"

"I don't know why everyone says that," Chance said. "She hardly ever drinks. What did you say about her dad?"

"Never mind. I was confusing her with someone else."

I yanked the ruler out of the door handles and made my escape from the stairwell. I couldn't believe how badly I'd screwed that up. Halfway down the hallway, the realization hit me that it could have been worse—much worse. I'd nearly blown everything just because I let myself get all jealous of some other guy. I'd nearly spilled everything.

25

There are approximately two million things that could go wrong, but I don't want to think about that. I prefer to focus on the positive, like the fact that a new chapter in our lives is about to begin, that the whole future is out there waiting for us. I used to know a girl who would have called these negatives. Sometimes the thing about growing up is that it allows us to see the world in a whole new way.

Standing in Hamilton's kitchen, I survey the oversized bags of chips and popcorn covering her kitchen table. I warned her she was still hosting her annual end-of-the-year bash, but I didn't give her a whole lot of specifics.

"I don't think you got enough chips," I say.

"Just how many people did you put on the guest list?"

"Well, everyone."

"Everyone?"

"The entire school."

"Alex! Where are we going to put everyone?"

"It's a nice night. There's plenty of room in the backyard."

I glance in her direction, hoping for a smile, but it's still that blank, vacant look. I have a hard time getting used to it. She doesn't really even look like Hamilton ... that's because she isn't Hamilton, not anymore. She's Janey. I don't really know Janey. The truth is, Janey makes me uncomfortable. I don't know how to act around her.

I didn't put Janey's name on the guest list. I should have. And even though it's completely wrong, a small part of me wishes she was the way she used to be. I long to hear Olivia's voice, or see Nordica blush when I look in her direction. I have a feeling that no one from the clique will be here tonight. It feels strange. Technically, this party is being thrown by a girl who no longer exists.

I know it's all for the best. I try telling myself this, but it doesn't erase that empty feeling inside me.

"You don't think it might be overkill?" she says, meaning my all-inclusive guest list.

"It's the last party," I point out. "I mean, it's only fair to give everyone a chance to attend."

"This is going to be a disaster," she says, with a roll of her eyes.

As folks begin to arrive, a knot forms in my stomach. I catch myself, at more than one point, holding my breath. I keep expecting someone to do something or say something that will make Hamilton-Janey fall apart, but nothing like that happens. She's remarkably cool with the river of people flooding into the house. She doesn't really seem like Hamilton, but she doesn't seem like a mental patient, either. I doubt that anyone else notices the change in her. They're too busy being happy and celebratory. Besides, it's not like they were ever too observant of her personality changes before.

Things are going smoothly so far, so why do I feel like some sort of mad scientist who's created a monster? Janey isn't a monster. She's a sweet girl, although she'll never be the girl I used to know. It frightens me to think I've lost her forever. But then, I recall how frightening it was to see that girl self-destructing before my eyes.

I'm there by her side when Chance finds us on the patio. He's wearing one of his stupid grins.

"Great party," he says to her.

"I really didn't have much to do with it," she says. "But thanks." Her words are innocent enough, but the tone in which they are uttered, the phrasing, something about it reminds me of Olivia. I tense up, and I can't help but notice the way Chance eyes me warily.

"You're being too modest," I tell her. "This party's been four years in the making." She half smiles at this, and Chance offers up a good-natured chuckle.

"Well, I just wanted to say thanks," Chance says. "For everything. And I'm glad that you're doing better."

She nods, still wearing that half smile. I'm relieved when Chance starts to head back to the party, but that relief melts when she calls out to him. She looks suddenly serious. He spins around.

"You're a good guy," she says. Her voice falters slightly, and I move closer to her, ready to whisk her away if need be. "I used to know a girl who liked you. It was an ill-fated sort of thing, never meant to be, but in another life, you know, maybe it would have been different."

"Sure," he says. He doesn't look all that puzzled. Does he know? Did he know all along? Does it matter? His next words dispel all my doubts. "I used to know a guy who liked you, too," he says. "But there were complications and commitments that got in the way. I'm sure, in another life, you two would have gotten together."

She nods. The half smile reappears. Chance shoots me a friendly wave before disappearing into the crowd.

"You can stop that now," she says to me.

"What?"

"The jealous boyfriend act."

I wonder if that's what I am. Am I her boyfriend? How can I be, when I don't even know this stranger? I stare at her, but her face is unreadable.

"I'll be right back," I tell her.

The backyard is thick with kids. I fight my way through the crowds and find a dark, deserted corner near the shed. I sit down, resting against the shed's rough, wood-panel wall. When I decided to throw this party I was worried it might be too much for her, but I'm the one who can't handle it. I wanted to see Hamilton come alive with the excitement of the party, but Hamilton is gone and I don't know what to make of who she is now, of Janey. I feel dizzy, stuck with this weird impostor. Even as I think that,

I realize I have it backwards. The girl I used to know was the impostor.

"I can see why she used to do the guest list thing."

The voice startles me, and I jerk my head back, slamming it against the shed wall.

"Jasmine? What are you doing here?"

"You put my name on the list, remember?"

"I mean, why aren't you out there enjoying the party?"

"Too many people," she says. "It's overwhelming."

At least I'm not the only one feeling overwhelmed, even if our reasons are completely different.

"What are you doing out here?" she asks.

"I don't really know anyone here," I say. I expect her to laugh at this, but she doesn't. In fact, she's so quiet I'm not sure she's still here. "Jasmine?"

"Did you tell her about that newspaper article?" she asks.

"No, not yet," I say. Instead, I cling to the hope that she already knows her stepfather is dead.

"Maybe it would help her to have closure," Jasmine says.

And maybe it would send her completely off the deep end, I think. That's the thing. I feel like I have to tiptoe around her, never sure of what I should or shouldn't say.

"She isn't really the same," I say.

"But that's a good thing, isn't it? I mean, she was pretty messed up before, right?"

Sure, she was messed up before, but she's still messed up. She's just a different sort of messed up. Probably she'll never be completely right. I wonder how much Jasmine knows, and I realize I'm not worried. It doesn't matter anymore. It's okay if Jasmine knows. It's okay if everyone knows.

"I knew for a long time," I tell Jasmine. "I knew she had problems, and I didn't do a thing to try to help her. Instead, I helped her keep her secret hidden. I don't know if that makes me a horrible person or not."

"It makes you human. We all do dumb things from time to time."

"Even though I knew she was crazy, she didn't really seem crazy. She seemed like someone who had it all together."

"Everyone else seemed to think so."

"Exactly," I say, glad to hear her confirm what I've always believed. "She'd figured out a way to make it work, and people liked her the way she was. I liked her the way she was. And now, look at her. You can't say that how she is now is an improvement."

Jasmine studies me. "Alex, she was seriously screwed up. I mean, I can understand you didn't know what to do, but that doesn't mean not doing anything was right. She needed help. You realize that, right?"

"Like this school isn't full of people trying to be someone they aren't, playing roles so other people will like them."

"That's different," Jasmine says. She's pissed at me. I wonder if I've just lost the closest thing I've had to a friend. I do seem to have a knack for that sort of thing.

"Do you think it's my fault that she's like this now? Because I didn't do anything before?" I don't wait for her to answer. "I don't see why it has to be all my responsibility. What about everyone else? Her teachers, her friends, her mother? If they had taken the time to really get to know her, they would have known something was wrong with her."

"Chill," Jasmine says. "Look, she's been screwed up for a pretty long time, so it's not like saying something sooner would really have made that big of a difference."

She's right, of course. It makes me feel a little bit better. It's all right if she thinks I should have acted sooner; I deserve the blame. It actually feels somewhat better to accept the blame. It's not that I feel good—I don't. But I do feel like things are settled. It reminds me of what Jasmine said about closure.

"I have to go," I tell her.

The printout of the newspaper story is in my jacket pocket, and my jacket is hanging over the chair in Hamilton's—no, Janey's—kitchen. I have to fight my way through the crowds to retrieve it, then fight my way back through the crowds to locate Janey. Either she already knows all this and it won't matter, or finding out that her stepfather is dead might bring her another step or two closer to being a whole person. I ignore the third possibility, the one where this newspaper story completely undoes her. I've seen her in action tonight, and I know she's stronger than that.

"You're still here," she says. "I thought you left."

"I wanted to show you something," I say. I unfold the

printout and hand it to her. I watch her face as she reads it, and there's the briefest flicker of some emotion. It's gone too quickly for me to tell exactly what she was feeling.

"Why did you give this to me?" she asks. She doesn't sound upset in any way. She doesn't sound anything.

"I thought you would feel better knowing this," I explain. "He's dead."

"I think I tried telling you that," she says.

I recall Zelda that day outside the mall, the hot sun beating down on us. What had she said? Something about Hamilton's mother making Tom move out or sending him away or something like that ... no, she'd said *she made him go away.*

In my head, I hear Zelda saying the words, and I hear something I didn't hear before. It's something in her tone, the inflection in her voice. And I can almost hear Mrs. Best telling her daughter she'd made the bad man go away.

Zelda wasn't talking about Hamilton's stepfather leaving Fidelity. She was talking about him leaving the mortal plane.

I feel like an idiot for handing her the newspaper story. She didn't need my stupid bit of research to give her closure. She'd known all along what had become of her stepfather. No wonder she was so messed up.

"Your mother killed him," I say. I give her several seconds to refute this, but she doesn't. "No wonder she didn't want you to go to therapy. She let you become someone else, several someone elses, to save her own neck."

"I already told you, she didn't know." Her tone is sharp

and angry. I'm glad to see her expressing an emotion, even if it's a negative one directed at me. I don't entirely believe her. I mean, she may think she had her mother completely fooled, but how completely out of it would the woman have to have been not to notice what was really going on with her own child?

She hands the printout back to me. I don't want it, but I take it from her and shove it into my pocket.

She stands there looking out over the crowd milling around the backyard. There's something about that defiant stare that makes me think of Zelda. It's nothing but a passing flicker of recognition, but it makes me wonder. Maybe they aren't completely gone. Maybe there are still bits and fragments of her old selves in Janey.

It reminds me that I don't really know anything about Janey. Maybe it's time to fix that.

"I don't think we've been properly introduced," I say. "I'm Alex Journer." I hold out my hand for her to shake.

She stares down at it in confusion, then finally shakes my hand.

"Janey Best," she says. I expect the name that rolls so naturally off her lips to feel like nails on a chalkboard, but I must be getting used to it. It actually doesn't sound so bad. It has a nice ring to it.

"So, I don't know, maybe we could go out some time, get to know each other a bit better?"

"Sure, Alex. I'd like that," she says. A smile dances across her face, too quickly, but while it was there, she looked a lot like a girl I used be in love with.

Acknowledgments

Thank you to everyone who made this book possible and supported me on my writing journey, including all my friends and family, but most especially my parents, Robert and Carolyn Grosso. You guys rock! I would not have gotten to where I am today without your support.

I want to thank everyone at Flux for all their hard work in bringing this book to print. Special thanks to Brian Farrey, editor extraordinaire, who rescued this book from the slush pile and saw its potential. Thank you to editor Sandy Sullivan, whose sharp eyes and good ear have helped to clean up my sometimes incomprehensible and clunky prose. Thank you to the designers, the publicists, and the sales staff at Flux, who have helped me share my novel with the world.

Finally, thank you to the greater writing community, whose moral support, blog posts, and tweets have been there to help me in my writing journey. I am thankful to be a part of the Elevensies; I don't know where I would be without this wonderful support network. Also, a big, huge thank you to the Class of 2K11—I am so happy to make this writing journey with you. You guys are the best!

JAICO PUBLISHING HOUSE

Elevate Your Life. Transform Your World.

ESTABLISHED IN 1946, Jaico Publishing House is home to world-transforming authors such as Sri Sri Paramahansa Yogananda, Osho, The Dalai Lama, Sri Sri Ravi Shankar, Robin Sharma, Deepak Chopra, Jack Canfield, Eknath Easwaran, Devdutt Pattanaik, Khushwant Singh, John Maxwell, Brian Tracy and Stephen Hawking.

Our late founder Mr. Jaman Shah first established Jaico as a book distribution company. Sensing that independence was around the corner, he aptly named his company Jaico ('Jai' means victory in Hindi). In order to service the significant demand for affordable books in a developing nation, Mr. Shah initiated Jaico's own publications. Jaico was India's first publisher of paperback books in the English language.

While self-help, religion and philosophy, mind/body/spirit, and business titles form the cornerstone of our non-fiction list, we publish an exciting range of travel, current affairs, biography, and popular science books as well. Our renewed focus on popular fiction is evident in our new titles by a host of fresh young talent from India and abroad. Jaico's recently established Translations Division translates selected English content into nine regional languages.

Jaico's Higher Education Division (HED) is recognized for its student-friendly textbooks in Business Management and Engineering which are in use countrywide.

In addition to being a publisher and distributor of its own titles, Jaico is a major national distributor of books of leading international and Indian publishers. With its headquarters in Mumbai, Jaico has branches and sales offices in Ahmedabad, Bangalore, Bhopal, Bhubaneswar, Chennai, Delhi, Hyderabad, Kolkata and Lucknow.

SINCE 1946